Dragonfly Summer

DRAGONFLY SUMMER

Smith Mountain Lake Series - Book Two

Inglath Cooper

Contents

Copyright

Published by Fence Free Entertainment, LLC

Dragonfly Summer / Inglath Cooper

Fence Free Entertainment, LLC
Fence.free.entertainment.llc@gmail.com

Books by Inglath Cooper

Swerve
The Heart That Breaks
My Italian Lover
Fences – Book Three – Smith Mountain Lake Series
Dragonfly Summer – Book Two – Smith Mountain Lake Series
Blue Wide Sky – Book One – Smith Mountain Lake Series
That Month in Tuscany
And Then You Loved Me
Down a Country Road
Good Guys Love Dogs
Truths and Roses
Nashville – Part Ten – Not Without You
Nashville – Book Nine – You, Me and a Palm Tree
Nashville – Book Eight – R U Serious
Nashville – Book Seven – Commit
Nashville – Book Six – Sweet Tea and Me
Nashville – Book Five – Amazed
Nashville – Book Four – Pleasure in the Rain
Nashville – Book Three – What We Feel
Nashville – Book Two – Hammer and a Song
Nashville – Book One – Ready to Reach
On Angel's Wings
A Gift of Grace
RITA® Award Winner John Riley's Girl
A Woman With Secrets
Unfinished Business

A Woman Like Annie
The Lost Daughter of Pigeon Hollow
A Year and a Day

Reviews

"If you like your romance in New Adult flavor, with plenty of ups and downs, oh-my, oh-yes, oh-no, love at first sight, trouble, happiness, difficulty, and follow-your-dreams, look no further than extraordinary prolific author Inglath Cooper. Ms. Cooper understands that the romance genre deserves good writing, great characterization, and true-to-life settings and situations, no matter the setting. I recommend you turn off the phone and ignore the doorbell, as you're not going to want to miss a moment of this saga of the girl who headed for Nashville with only a guitar, a hound, and a Dream in her heart." – **Mallory Heart Reviews**

"Truths and Roses . . . so sweet and adorable, I didn't want to stop reading it. I could have put it down and picked it up again in the morning, but I didn't want to." – **Kirkusreviews.com**

On Truths and Roses: "I adored this book...what romance should be, entwined with real feelings, real life and roses blooming. Hats off to the author, best book I have read in a while." – **Rachel Dove, FrustratedYukkyMommyBlog**

"I am a sucker for sweet love stories! This is definitely one of those! It was a very easy, well written, book. It was easy to follow, detailed, and didn't leave me hanging without answers." – **www.layfieldbaby.blogspot.com**

"I don't give it often, but I am giving it here – the sacred 10. Why? Inglath Cooper's A GIFT OF GRACE mesmerized me; I consumed it in one sitting. When I turned the last page, it was three in the morning." – **MaryGrace Meloche, Contemporary Romance Writers**

5 Blue Ribbon Rating! ". . .More a work of art than a story. . .Tragedies affect entire families as well as close loved ones, and this story portrays that beautifully as well as giving the reader hope that somewhere out there is A GIFT OF GRACE for all of us." — **Chrissy Dionne, Romance Junkies 5 Stars**

"A warm contemporary family drama, starring likable people coping with tragedy and triumph." 4 1/2 Stars. — Harriet Klausner

"A GIFT OF GRACE is a beautiful, intense, and superbly written novel about grief and letting go, second chances and coming alive again after devastating adversity. Warning!! A GIFT OF GRACE is a three-hanky read...better make that a BIG box of tissues read! Wowsers, I haven't cried so much while reading a book in a long long time...Ms. Cooper's skill makes A GIFT OF GRACE totally believable, totally absorbing...and makes Laney Tucker vibrantly alive. This book will get into your heart and it will NOT let go. A GIFT OF GRACE is simply stunning in every way—brava, Ms. Cooper! Highly, highly recommended!" – 4 1/2 Hearts — Romance Readers Connection

"...A WOMAN WITH SECRETS...a powerful love story laced with treachery, deceit and old wounds that will not heal...enchanting tale...weaved with passion, humor, broken hearts and a commanding love that will have your heart soaring and cheering for a happily-ever-after love. Kate is strong-willed, passionate and suffers a bruised heart. Cole is sexy, stubborn and also suffers a bruised heart...gripping plot. I look forward to reading more of Ms. Cooper's work!" – **www.freshfiction.com**

*

May you touch dragonflies and stars,
dance with fairies and talk to the moon,
May you grow up with love and gracious hearts
and people who care.
– Author Unknown

*

Things do not change; we change.
– Henry David Thoreau

Keegan

I BELIEVE IT was architect Frank Lloyd Wright who said if you tip the world over on its side, everything loose will land in Los Angeles.

If that's so, then everything rooted and stable resides in Virginia.

At least that's how I remember it. As well as memories formed at eight years old can be remembered. I had experienced Virginia for two weeks during a summer camp I was chosen to attend with other city-bound foster kids.

The camp had been held on a farm at Smith Mountain Lake. That week had opened a door to another world for me, a world where people didn't exist for the next fix, the next high. Where children had value beyond being a bargaining chip for drug money.

That summer had provided me with amazing memories that I still draw on today as the picture of what life can look like when it's going as it should.

But then how long has it been since anything in my life looked as it should?

And what if this place I'm running to has become every bit as random and merciless as the city I just left? The place where I've spent the past twenty years of my life working toward something I truly thought I would eventually reach, only to realize I had been there all along. And never recognized it. Never valued it.

We still have a couple of hours to go before we reach Smith Mountain Lake. I glance across the seat at my sleeping son and wonder if I should wake him so he doesn't miss the incredible views as we travel through Charlottesville with its Blue Ridge Mountain backdrop.

I had considered making a stop at Monticello, Thomas Jefferson's home, taking an hour or so to tour the grounds, which I have heard are beautiful.

But Evan wouldn't want to, and if I'm honest, we'd both simply be going through the motions. Saying words just to fill the space, maintain the appearance that we both try to maintain every day. Moving forward without looking back. Trying to take notice of what good there is in front of us. Mostly, failing miserably.

The mountain between us is Reece. Evan's certainty that I could have prevented her from cutting us out of her life. My guilt that he is right.

So I let him sleep. Rolling down the window of the Range Rover and sticking my head out long enough to blow the need to sleep from my own brain.

I've been driving since five a.m. Almost twelve hours. Evan has offered to drive numerous times, but I've insisted that I'm fine. It's crazy not to let him relieve me and not something I can even explain, beyond the fact that I feel the need to get us to this new life on my own.

I'm the one, after all, who kept us in a life we should have left six or seven years ago when I started to see the fallout of remaining in L.A. Continuing to work in a career that fosters the perception that problems can be recognized and resolved in forty-two minute episodes.

I had years to recognize and process those going on in my own house. And I failed in the biggest way it is possible to fail. I failed my child.

South of Charlottesville on 29, the road dips and curves a bit more. I pass a couple of state troopers parked in the middle of the highway and check my speed.

The pull of the brakes rouses Evan. He lifts his head and gives me a groggy stare. "Everything all right?"

"Yeah," I say. "Just trying not to get a ticket."

"How long before we get there?"

"Less than two hours. Are you hungry?"

"Nah."

"We can stop if you are."

"I'm fine, Mom," he says with the edge in his voice that has become more and more the norm.

I decide that silence is the best response and reach out to turn up the music playing from my iPhone through Bluetooth.

Evan manages to turn his back to me, even though he is six-two and wearing a seat belt. His rejection stings. But I don't blame him.

If I could reject myself, I would.

The best things in life are unexpected – because there were no expectations.
– Eli Khamarov

Bowie

SOMETIMES, I THINK it has to be a sin, this life I'm living.

If not a sin, then at least something I'm probably not deserving of.

I'm sitting on the front porch of the house my grandparents built on prime Virginia farm land in the late 1940s. It's big, way too big for me to be living here alone. But I love its Southern two-story charm. The porches that rim the upper and lower levels. The two enormous oak trees that throw evening shade across the green yard that leads down to the dock and the edge of the lake. The 130 acres that surrounds it and provides a physical boundary from neighbors getting too close.

I love this time of day too. Not quite dark yet, but still light enough that I can watch the boats idling across the wide stretch of Smith Mountain Lake before me. It's the peacefulness that drew me here, that keeps me here.

It's the thing I crave most in life now. Peace. Hard to believe when all I used to want was the next case with all its uncertainty and conflict. The emotional noise of another criminal wrong I was determined to rectify.

Two years of living in this house by myself have not made me lonely. Or want for regular human company.

At my feet, Carson rolls over on his back, paws in the air. He struggles to get footing, and I wonder if he is dreaming about swimming or running, both of which he loves. I reach down and scratch his belly. He groans, opens an eye to make sure it's me and goes back to his dreaming.

He's a questionable blend of Black Lab and most likely Australian cattle dog. If he's not wanting to dive off the end of the dock forty times a day, he's trying to temper his genetic need to herd me from one end of the farm to the other. His inner conflicts are a good deal like my own, except that he can indulge both without too much fallout.

The same is not true for me. I had to make a choice between mine.

Despite his bossiness, his is about the only company I care to have on a regular basis these days. I'm not sure whether this says more about my love for the canine species or my disillusion with human beings. Most likely both.

I glance at my MacBook Air, reading the last paragraph I wrote to remind myself where I left off before my thoughts started to wander. I focus on the screen and start up with the story again.

I write for an hour or so, forgetting about the boats on the lake in front of me, the salad I meant to go inside and fix. I even manage to block out Carson's snoring, because I'm there in the world I'm creating out of nothing with people I force to face their obstacles and fears, instead of running away from them.

It's the sound of a car and the flash of headlights that pulls me back to reality. It's completely dark now, the occasional red light of a passing boat on the lake all I can make out.

I put the laptop on the table next to my chair. Carson gets to his feet and throws out a warning bark, trotting off in front of me with his fur raised. I follow him to the side of the house where a vehicle sits with its engine running. I can't tell if I know who it is or not because the headlights are shining directly at me.

I walk to an angle where I can make out the fact that it's a Range Rover with California plates.

The driver's door opens, and a woman gets out. "I'm sorry," she says. "I'm afraid I've gotten a little lost. My cell service is sketchy so the GPS has given up. Can you possibly tell me where Walker Road is?"

Carson is barking full force now, doing a near-perfect imitation of a trained security dog. We both know better. Despite his herding instincts, a loud boo will send him running. "It's all right, Carson," I say, patting my leg. He trots over and sits up against me.

The woman's expression reveals concern and uncertainty. I relieve her with, "He's harmless."

It's clear she doesn't believe me. She grips the door of the vehicle and says, "I won't keep you. Do you know Walker Road?"

"I do," I say, noticing then that she's pretty. And lost, I remind myself. "Ah, if you go back out my driveway and take a right, you'll need to go about two miles. Hang a left when you pass the tennis court and another right at the Corner Country Store."

I realize I've turned into one of the locals whose direction-giving skills I once ridiculed. She looks more than confused, shaking her head with, "Could you say that again, please?"

I walk closer to the vehicle, now able to fully make out her features. Long, blondish hair pulled back in a messy ponytail. She's fairly tall and thin, her face hollowed with angles that either make her an athlete or someone who's not a big fan of eating. Something about her seems vaguely familiar, but that's unlikely with the California plates.

I go over the directions again, and when I'm done, she still doesn't seem all that sure about her ability to find her way there. "I can lead you over if you'd like."

As soon as the words are out, I have no idea where they came from. I do not make a habit of interacting with people in general, much less a stranger who just pulled up in my driveway.

"If you don't mind, that would be great," she says, looking instantly relieved.

I notice then that there appears to be someone in the passenger seat. I lean my head to the right for a better view, and she says, "My son. He's asleep. We've been driving for the past few days."

"Straight through?" I ask, glancing at the plates.

"With a couple of short stops," she says.

When she doesn't elaborate, I say, "I'll get my keys. Be right back."

Carson follows me inside where I grab the key from the bowl by the front door. I lock the house and walk to the truck, waiting for Carson to jump in before saying to the woman, "Just follow us."

"Thank you so much," she says, looking truly appreciative, and adding, "It's 4211 Walker Road."

"Got it," I say.

She gets in the Range Rover and waits for me to turn around, then pulls out behind me.

I don't bother speeding on the narrow roads leading to the address. I think for a moment of how I used to drive in northern Virginia, nineteen miles over the freeway speed limit when I could get away with it. Twenty was a reckless driving ticket so I stayed just short of that. I had always been in such a hurry. Had to get there faster. So I could get more done. Faster, more. Faster, more. Until I finally hit a wall that made me question what the hell I had been in such a hurry for. Because it didn't really matter when I got there. Whatever wrong I managed to semi-right, the next day would simply hold another one.

Carson sits up in the passenger seat, his nose pressing through the crack in the window, assessing the night smells.

We make the turn onto Walker Road, and I slow down to let my headlights glance across the mailbox numbers. 4201. Another half-mile to 4211. I flip on the blinker, intent on turning around to head back. She pulls in behind me, so I continue down the driveway looking for a place to pull over and let her pass.

There isn't one until I get to the house, and, by now, it feels like politeness would dictate that I wish her luck or something.

The house is beautiful. Apparently new, judging from the window manufacturer stickers still on the glass panes. The style is something between French and contemporary, two stories with an enormous arched entrance. Definitely one of the pricier pieces of real estate currently on the market. But then if she moved here from California, this probably seemed like a deal.

She gets out of the Rover and walks over to the truck door. She stops at my lowered window and says, "I can't thank you enough. It's just so good to finally be here."

I can hear the relief in her voice. And I see, now that she's so close, she's even prettier than I had realized. I feel myself fumble a little for words. Tongue-tied? Seriously.

"Ah, you're welcome. Glad to help."

The passenger door to the Range Rover opens, and a very tall teenage boy climbs out. "Mom?"

"We're here, hon," she says, glancing over her shoulder. "Come and meet—" She breaks off there and adds, "I'm sorry. We didn't get each other's name."

"Bowie Dare," I say.

"I'm Keegan Monroe," she says. "And this is my son, Evan."

Evan is standing by his mom now, towering over her, actually. He sticks out his hand, unexpectedly polite. "Nice to meet you," he says.

"Mr. Dare helped us find the house. I got a little lost the last few miles."

"You should have woken me up," he says, the words accusing.

"You've got the keys to the place?" I ask.

"Yes," she says. "We should be all set."

"I'll wait if you want to make sure you can get in. If your cell phone isn't working, you might have trouble getting help if the key doesn't work."

Evan gives me a long look, as if he's used to men hitting on his mother. Am I? Hitting on her?

"Or I can just go," I say quickly. "I'm sure you'll have it under control."

"Actually," she says, reaching out to put a hand on my arm. "If you don't mind waiting a minute, that would be great. The thought of spending a night in the car is actually a little nauseating right at the moment."

Evan settles his gaze on her hand, and she quickly pulls it back.

"Sure," I say, cutting the truck engine. "I'll just wait here."

"Thank you," she says, walking to the Rover and pulling her purse from the back seat.

She carries it with her to the front door, while Evan waits by the truck with me.

"What kind of dog?" he asks, ducking his head to look at Carson.

"The spoiled kind," I say.

Carson thumps his tail against the seat, no doubt recognizing the label.

"That's the best kind," Evan says. "I've always wanted a dog."

"Noticed the California plates," I say. "Not as easy to have one out there, I guess."

"Not really. Lots of people have them. Mom's just always been kind of scared of them."

"Ah," I say, as if I understand. "That's a shame."

"I'll have one someday. When I have my own place."

"The key works," his mom calls out from the front door. She steps in and turns on the outside lights. The house looks instantly inviting.

"All right, then," I say. "I'll be heading home."

"Do you know the lake pretty well?" Evan asks, as if he's not ready for me to go.

"Yeah," I say. "I spent a lot of time on the lake when I was a kid and moved here for good about two years ago."

"From what I've read, there's not an awful lot to do."

"I guess that depends on what you like. Are you in school?"

"One more year of high school."

"That should keep you busy," I say.

"Mom wants to homeschool me," he says, his tone exuding extreme disapproval.

"I'm sure she must have a good reason," I say, even as I realize I have no way of knowing whether her reasons are good or not.

She's back at the front door now, waving at us. "The Realtor left us a bottle of good champagne. Can you join us for a minute, Mr. Dare?"

"We should be going," I say, tipping my head at Carson, who's standing in the truck seat and wagging his tail in disagreement.

"Come on," Evan says. "One toast, and we'll let you leave."

I consider arguing, but find myself at least a little curious. Maybe I'm more in need of human company than I realized. "Okay," I say. "One toast."

I get out of the truck, telling Carson I'll be right back.

"He can come in," Evan says.

"Your mom might not like that. New floors and all."

"She doesn't dislike dogs. She's just scared of them." He turns to his mom and calls out, "Okay if he brings Carson in too?"

She nods, and I'm not sure whether her expression is one of politeness or fear, but rather than argue, I open the door and Carson hops out.

We follow Evan inside, stepping onto the marble floors of the foyer. "I think the kitchen is this way," he says, taking the hall to our left. He's right, and his mom is already there, opening a very large bottle of champagne with a French label. The Realtor must have been extremely appreciative of the sale.

"Beautiful house," I say, glancing around the room and taking in the mahogany cabinets, Viking stove and refrigerator.

"Thanks," she says, popping the cork. The sound makes Carson bark, which in turn makes her jump.

"Carson," I say. "Come here, boy."

"It's okay," she says. "I'm a little jumpy, I guess."

She opens the sleeve of plastic champagne glasses, pulls out three and lines them up on the counter. She pours two full ones and a half one, which I'm guessing is for Evan.

"Mom," Evan says.

"I could get arrested," she says. "You're not legal."

He rolls his eyes and reaches for the glass.

"Hold on," she says. "We have to make a toast."

There's something in her voice I can't quite put my finger on. Determination? Resignation? Those two things don't have a lot in common, so I'm guessing I'm off the mark.

She passes me a glass and holds hers in the air. "To forging new paths. Making a fresh start. Looking ahead instead of back."

She taps her glass against mine and then Evan's.

Evan doesn't meet her gaze but downs the contents of his glass in a single gulp. She throws him a worried glance before taking a sip of her own.

I try mine, and the taste lives up to the label. "Very nice," I say and then finish it, setting the plastic cup on the counter. "Thank you. And I have to be going. I hope you both get a good night's sleep."

"Thanks," they say in unison. Maybe it's just my imagination, but it feels as if they're both searching for a reason to keep me here, but neither voices it.

"Come on, Carson," I say. "Better get you home before you turn into a pumpkin."

"Maybe we'll see you around the lake," Evan says, and I'm thinking he's lonely. Which leads me to say, "Drop by the dock if you're out and about." Which is not something I am prone to saying.

"We will," Evan says.

"Thank you again, Mr. Dare," his mom says.

"It's Bowie," I say. "And you're welcome." And then I think *Keegan*. That's her name. Keegan.

It's not until Carson and I are a mile or so down the road toward home when the full name comes to me. Keegan Monroe. And the television series. *Aimless*. Keegan Monroe. The actress.

I look at Carson and say, "She probably thinks we've been living under a rock, huh?"

Carson barks and wags his tail.

"Yeah, I agree. I like our rock."

*

It is the sweet, simple things of life which are the real ones after all.

– Laura Ingalls Wilder

Keegan

WE HAVE NO furniture yet, but I don't even care. I'm just so glad to finally be here.

I unpack what food we still have in our cooler, put it in the refrigerator and then go outside to get the blankets I brought along from the back of the car. The moving truck is supposed to arrive tomorrow, but a makeshift bed on the floor tonight actually sounds like heaven.

I pop the back of the Rover and reach inside for the blankets, and then go still for a moment at a sound I don't recognize. It's chirping. Crickets? Birds? Frogs? Frogs, I think. I remember reading about the frogs you can hear at night around Smith Mountain Lake when I was researching the area and deciding whether this was the place for Evan and me. I liked the idea of hearing them at night. I'm so used to the sound of traffic and the constant noise of a city. The thought of singing frogs seemed pure and innocent.

I lower the tailgate and sit on it, closing my eyes and listening until it begins to sound like actual music. There's a rhythm and a cadence, and it just hits me how ready I am for this new life. How tired I have become of chaos and competition and criticism.

I stare out into the dark night, another thing I'm not used

to. In the city, there's always light. Streetlights. Skyscrapers with lights shining from every floor at all hours. There's never total darkness. Unlike here. It felt strange driving along the country roads and going a mile or more without seeing a single house lit up. This isn't a life I've ever lived, and I wonder if I'll end up regretting what I've done. Moving my son across the country. Backing out of a contract for a still successful series.

From here on an early summer Virginia night, with nothing but crickets and darkness surrounding me, it's easy to start thinking that maybe I've made a mistake. Maybe I should have stuck it out. Gambled on Evan turning out nothing like Reece. But then a year ago, would I have dreamed that Reece would take the path she's taken?

No.

Did I see any of it coming?

No.

It's not as if I really had a choice about leaving L.A. I've lost one child to something I've hated my whole life. The thing that destroyed my childhood and made me vow that my own children would never know what it was like to live that life. And now Reece has chosen it. I can't lose Evan to it as well.

"Mom?"

"Out here, Ev," I call back.

He walks from the house to the car, barefoot and shirtless. "What are you doing?"

"Just listening for a bit."

"To what?"

"The night sounds."

"I don't hear anything," he says, looking at me as if he's wondering about my mental health.

"Frogs," I say.

"Is that what that is?"

"Pretty, isn't it?"

"I guess. I prefer the purr of Maseratis on Sunset Boulevard."

"Ev."

"Just sayin'."

I pat the tailgate, inviting him to sit. He does so, reluctantly. "Are you going to give this place a chance?" I ask.

He shrugs a defiant teenager shrug. "You know I didn't want to move here. You didn't give me a choice."

"And you know why I did that."

"Because you think I'm going to turn out like Reece. Why can't you just trust me to be me?"

I glance off for a moment, before forcing myself to look at him. "I do trust you, Evan. But the life we led out there, it just does something to kids your age. It's not real. It's like we lived in a plastic bubble, where it seems like you can get away with making bad choices. "

"That's rich, you know, coming from you. You've made a career creating worlds that aren't real. Worlds that people wish they lived in."

My son's accusation stings. I wish I could deny it, but I can't. Even so, I say, "Playing a role on TV and living one in real life are two different things."

He shrugs again, and I can't tell if he agrees or not.

"It's not your fault, you know," he says, looking at me now with something softer in his face, and I know he's talking about Reece.

"Yeah. It is."

"She's making her own choices. How can you be responsible for that?"

"I'm apparently something she utterly despises. And never

wants to be." My voice breaks here, and I hate myself for the emotion that is always at the surface of anything related to Reece's rejection of me. I wish I could harden myself to it, find a way for it not to hurt so damn much.

Evan reaches out and puts his hand over mine. He's not one to show physical affection, so the gesture has extra meaning to me.

"I don't think it's you, Mom. She's just consumed with lashing out at the world in general."

"Don't worry about it, Evan. Your only job right now is to be seventeen, finish your last year of high school and make some new friends here."

"How am I going to make friends if you homeschool me?"

"We'll look for activities you can get involved in."

"Activities? That sounds like I'm in first grade."

"Sports then. How's that?"

"You can't play football unless you go to the public high school."

"There are other sports."

"You know I love football."

"Sometimes, we have to make sacrifices, Evan," I say, instantly regretting the sharp note in my voice.

"Shouldn't Reece be the one making the sacrifice, Mom? She's the one who's blown our family to hell."

"Evan."

"Well, hasn't she?" He slides off the tailgate and faces me, rigid with anger. "And what are the repercussions for her? She's off doing whatever the hell she wants to. Exactly who is being punished?"

I reach out to put a hand on his arm, but he shakes me away.

"I get why you're so pissed at her," he says. "She's being a class-A bitch. But the problem is that everyone is paying for that except her."

He turns away then and walks back to the house, ignoring me when I call after him.

I jump when the front door slams behind him. I want to deny everything he's just said, but I can't. Because he's right.

Damn it. He's right.

*

When the boy is growing he has a wolf in his belly.
– German Proverb

Evan

SHIT. HOW AM I supposed to sleep on this wood floor with no pillow, no blanket?

I am NOT going back outside to ask Mom for them. I'll sleep in the bathtub first.

I lean against a bedroom wall, slide to the floor and close my eyes, trying not to think about how hard it's going to be to get through this next year. How unfair it is that I should even have to. I am suddenly so angry at Reece that I swear if she were in front of me right now, I'd have trouble stopping myself from strangling her.

Our whole life she's been the perfect child, and then she hits eighteen and decides to turn into Miss Queen of Rebellion. And because she's eighteen she can do whatever the hell she wants. While I'm here reaping the consequences of her behavior because Mom suddenly feels like she has to put a moat around the castle.

My phone buzzes. I pull it from my shirt pocket. Mandy on FaceTime. I start to refuse the call, not sure I'm up to talking to her right now, but the need to hear a familiar voice trumps.

"Hey," I say, looking into the phone screen.

"Hey, babe," she says. "Are you in the sticks yet?"

"Yeah, that's me," I say. "Stuck in the sticks."

She giggles. It's the only thing I don't like about her. That giggle. It's like she's not completely in control of it, and every once in a while, it just slips out, even at times when a giggle doesn't seem entirely appropriate. I focus on her face, her very pretty, California-tan face. "I miss you," I say, wanting it to be true.

"Not as much as I miss you," she says.

"Want to bet?"

"You'd lose."

"No, I wouldn't."

"That's sweet. In fact, so sweet that I think you deserve a reward."

"What did you have in mind?" I ask.

She lowers one side of her tank top, and then the other, until her shoulders are bare. "Should I stop here?" she asks, innocence underlining each word.

"No," I say, feeling that familiar catch in my throat. "Definitely not."

She shimmies the top down her sides, revealing a lacy black bra. "How about here?"

"You're going to kill me, you know."

She giggles again. Nails on the chalkboard.

She releases the front hook of the bra, slips free of it and drops it to the floor. "How much are you missing me now?" she asks.

"You have no idea," I say. Was it just a few days ago that I didn't have to rely on a phone app to see what I very badly want to touch?

"Are you really going to be there a whole year, Evan?"

A year? It might as well be eternity.

*

Attraction isn't a choice.
– David DeAngelo

Bowie

I WRITE EARLY. Five to eight if it's a normal day.

Three hours usually gives me ten to twelve pages. I'm happy with that. It makes me feel productive, and yet I have so much of the day left to do other things.

But this morning, it's just not coming.

I've had three cups of coffee. It's almost seven-thirty, and I've barely written a hundred words.

Frustration rustles through me. By my own commitment, I have to sit here until the 2500 words are done.

It's been a long time since I had a day where the story wasn't there. But then in all honesty, the reason isn't hard to figure out.

I'm distracted. By the constant refrain of Keegan Monroe in my head. Just what I need.

I can hear Carson whine from the kitchen. I get up from my desk chair and go let him out, breaking my own rule and stepping outside into the June morning, where I immediately lose all desire to go back in the house.

Carson runs to the edge of the lake where he tries to herd a flock of uncooperative Canadian geese away from the dock. I give him points for his determined bark, but the geese aren't buying it and continue their bug hunting along the water's edge.

"A for effort," I call out to him. He wags his tail and wades into the water before swimming out to the floating dock fifty yards or so away and climbing up the slanted ramp I built for him. He shakes water from his coat and plops down to soak up some morning sun.

Most people would think that I've taught Carson a lot. He's a smart boy, and I've shown him all the basics that seem to convince others that he's "obedience-trained." He sits when I ask him, fetches the ball when I throw it, and rolls over for a belly rub when I snap my fingers.

But the truth is, Carson has taught me more than I'll ever teach him. Gratitude for instance. When I moved here two years ago, I wasn't sure if life would ever make sense to me again. I was lonely and alone, and it only took a few days for me to grow tired of hearing my own footsteps echoing in the house.

So I looked up the address for the local pound and drove out one afternoon during the time the website indicated it was open. The shelter sat next to the county landfill, and the irony of this did not escape me as I drove down the gravel road and parked in the lot outside the obviously outdated, underfunded building. The only other vehicle in the lot was an Animal Control truck. The driver's side door opened, and a uniformed officer stepped out.

"We're about to close for the day," he'd said, using his thumbs in his front belt loops to hitch up his pants. It was clear he wasn't happy to see me.

"I want to adopt a dog," I said.

"Can you come back on Monday?" Phrased as a question, it really wasn't.

"Why?"

"I'm the only one here, and I've got something in the back of the truck I need to take care of."

"I can wait," I said.

He definitely wanted to argue with me, but visibly forced himself not to. "Wait inside."

I did as he asked and walked into the building, leaving the door open for him. I heard the tailgate of the truck open and then slam shut. A few moments later, he walked in carrying a cardboard box.

"Dead puppies," he said, as if he wanted to shock me.

"What happened?" I asked, not sure I wanted to know the answer.

"Found them in a dumpster up on Grassy Hill."

"Someone actually put them in there?"

"Yeah," he said, and I heard the weary note in his voice, as if this were nothing new for him.

Just then, a whine sounded from the box, and a small black head raised up far enough that I could see it over the edge.

"Great," the officer said.

"There's one alive?" I asked.

"Yeah, but he won't last long. I'm going to put him out of his misery."

"What do you mean?"

"He won't live through the night. Euthanasia is the kindest thing I can do for him."

The part of me that respected authority, that realized he probably knew what he was talking about urged me to let it go. But then I took a step closer and looked into the box where that tiny puppy lay in the middle of its four dead siblings, and I just felt this rage that I couldn't explain. And I couldn't ignore.

"I'll take it," I said. "The puppy."

"It's not available for adoption."

"You're just going to end its life. Why can't I adopt it instead?"

"Because it's going to die anyway," he said with an edge to his voice.

I had the feeling then that we had entered the pride zone, and that he was now going to feel the need to make a point with me. I didn't care though. I wasn't leaving without the puppy.

I pulled my cell phone from my pocket. "Let me just check with the sheriff's office first. I'm pretty sure a willing adopter negates the option of euthanasia."

He let me get as far as hello, before he said, "Okay. The sick puppy is yours." He lifted the puppy from the box and basically shoved it at me.

The puppy whimpered, and I forced myself not to punch the jerk officer in the face. "Is there paperwork I need to fill out?" I asked, my jaw tight.

"He won't live long enough to justify paperwork," he said, walking down the hallway toward the back of the shelter and through a door, which he slammed behind him.

The puppy began to shiver, and I lifted up the bottom of my shirt to cover him. I used my phone to find the nearest vet, where we both spent a good part of the next two weeks. Him fighting to live. And me willing him to.

Watching him out on the dock now, rolling over to scratch his back on the rough wood, his paws up in the air, I think what a waste it would have been for his life to have been taken that afternoon.

But then innocent lives are lost every day in this world. Who knows this better than I? A man who walked away from a career where he could no longer witness it firsthand. A man who could now get no closer than writing about it.

*

There is a time to take counsel of your fears, and there is a time to never listen to any fear.
– George S. Patton

Keegan

THE MOVING TRUCK arrives at ten. I'm still on California time, and I don't wake up until I hear its engine growling up the driveway.

I drag myself out of my blanket cocoon and over to the window where the big white truck filled with everything I had thought meaningful enough to bring with us sits waiting.

I manage to run to the bathroom and brush my teeth before the doorbell sounds. I shimmy into jeans and a T-shirt, slip on a pair of Vans and run down the stairs. I open the door and find two burly men staring back at me through eyes that look in need of sleep. They are wearing uniform shirts with a name tag above the left pocket. Ted and Darren.

"Ms. Monroe?" Ted says.

"Yes," I say. "So glad you made it."

"Glad to be here," Darren agrees. "We can start unloading as soon as you'd like us to."

"Could I get you some coffee first?"

They both perk up at the question and thank me.

"It'll just take me a couple of minutes to get it going."

"We'll start opening up the truck then," Ted says, and they head back outside.

I manage to find the French press coffee maker I'd packed in the car, along with the ground coffee. The sink has a hot water dispenser, so I use it to fill the pot. I decide to call Evan down even though I know he would rather sleep. I remind myself that one of the reasons we moved here is so that he can live a more realistic life, one that doesn't include other people waiting on him all the time. Which means I need to ask him to help the movers rather than sleep while they do all the work.

"Evan?" I call from the bottom of the stairs. No answer. I call again. And then walk up to his room, cracking the door. "Evan?"

"What?" he responds in a grumpy voice.

"The movers are here. Time to unload the truck."

"Isn't that what they're here for?" he asks, raising up on an elbow to look at me if I've lost my last strand of sense.

"It is. And we're helping."

"Oh, for crap's sake, Mom! Can I just promise not to turn out like Reece? And if I do, will you stop making me the object of your parental experiment?"

"Your big toe is about one inch from being across the line," I advise him as sternly as I can manage. "Hop up, and let's get busy."

"Do I even get to eat first?"

"Coffee's ready. There's some food in the fridge."

With that, I head back downstairs, forcing myself to draw a deep breath and remember that he's seventeen. And acting out the same way he had when he was a toddler and I told him it was time for bed. Somehow, it was just easier to take from the toddler.

I pour coffee in paper cups for Ted and Darren and take

it outside to them. They seem grateful to have it and sip appreciatively.

"That's awfully good, ma'am," Darren says, tipping his head in thanks.

"I'm glad."

"You sure are a long way from L.A.," Ted says, glancing out at the view of Smith Mountain in the distance.

"I am that," I agree.

"My wife sure enjoyed your show," Darren says. "She hated to see you leave it. Especially in that car wreck and all."

I smile. "Grisly, wasn't it?"

"Wondered why they didn't just have you leave town for a while or something."

"I asked the writers to give me a permanent exit so I wouldn't be tempted to come back."

"Ah," they say, but look as if they have no idea what I'm talking about.

"It would have been tempting," I say. "Sort of like bringing that slice of cheesecake home from the restaurant where you have to look at in your refrigerator. If I leave it at the restaurant, no temptation."

"Most people wouldn't be able to bring themselves to leave an opportunity like that," Ted says.

"It's all in the motivation, I guess," I say, and then add, "I'll get my coffee, and we'll get started in a few minutes?"

"Sure thing," Darren says.

My motivation is leaning on the kitchen counter with his elbows locked and his eyes closed.

"Coffee?" I ask.

I take his mumble as a yes and pour him a cup. I make my own then and take a grateful sip.

I walk through the lower level of the house, opening

windows in an attempt to release the smell of paint and newly finished floors.

"This house isn't as nice as the one we had in L.A.," Evan calls out from the kitchen.

"I like this house," I call back. "It's comfortable. Not overwhelming."

"Small?"

"It's not small by most people's standards."

"So now we have to be most people?"

"Evan." By now I'm back in the kitchen. "You sound like a snob."

"I'm not a snob. I just very much happened to like the life we had in L.A. The life I had in L.A."

"It's one year, Ev. If you want to go back after that, I'm not going to stop you."

"Meanwhile, it's Homeschoolville for me in the boonies."

"If you choose to look at it that way."

"What other way is there to look at it?"

I hear my therapist's voice in my head. *Do not engage. Do not engage.* I drain the remainder of my coffee and head outside to the moving truck.

BY LATE AFTERNOON, the last piece of furniture has been brought into the house and put in place. Amazing, that in such a short time, the rooms have been completely transformed.

I only brought the pieces I really loved, things that have some sort of emotional connection for me. The house in L.A. had a contemporary feel to it. What I've put together here is much warmer, color a theme in every room. It feels more like a home, and I wonder why I let myself go along with the designer who had insisted on all that modern furniture and glass tables.

I walk to the window at the far side of the living room, staring out at the wide water view of the lake. Boats dip and dash across the surface. A MasterCraft pulls a skier who cuts back and forth across the wake with the skill of an expert, her shoulder nearly touching the surface with every turn.

It seems to be a theme of mine. Going along to get along. I hate conflict. Fussing. Upheaval. And so I guess I've made a habit of agreeing when I don't really agree. Except with Reece and this last battle of ours. My stomach grips with the thought, and I shut my eyes in an attempt to prevent it from hijacking my brain.

"Mom?" Evan calls out from the front door.

"Yeah?"

"We've finished loading up all the packing stuff. The mover guys want to know if you need anything else before they go?"

"No," I say, "but hold on a sec." I walk into the kitchen and pull four $100 bills from my wallet. I take them through the foyer where Evan is waiting with obvious impatience. "Would you give each of them $200?"

"I thought you paid the bill before we left," he says, looking down at the money.

"This is extra. For them," I say.

"Oh. Do I get extra?"

"Evan," I say, beginning to grow a little weary of his constant needling.

"Okay," he says and charges out the door, leaving attitude in his wake.

I knew when I made the decision to move us here that he would not make it easy for me. I wasn't wrong.

I go back in the kitchen and target the dishes on the counter as my next project. I unwrap the plates, then the cups and bowls. I'm stacking them in the cabinet next to the sink when Evan walks through, headed for the stairs.

"Do you want a snack?" I call after him.

"I'm not five, Mom."

"I didn't say you were five. I asked if you wanted a snack."

"I'm going for a run," he says.

"Where?"

"Just down the road," he says, stopping at the foot of the stairs to throw me a glare. "Is that okay?"

"It's fine, Evan. Just be careful."

He takes the steps two at a time, and then I hear his door slam. I flinch at the sound, rubbing my hand across the back of my neck and sighing.

My phone buzzes on the countertop. I walk over and glance at the screen, start to pick it up, pull my hand back and then reach for it again.

"Hey, Joseph," I say, putting the phone to my ear.

"Have you reached the edge of the earth yet?" he asks, with notable sarcasm.

"Virginia is hardly the edge of the earth," I say.

"For all intents and purposes, it might as well be."

"In case you really were concerned, I am in my house, furniture in place."

"You don't waste time."

"I'm ready to be settled. The last few months have felt anything but."

"No one made you uproot your life and drive it across the country."

"Joseph, if you're calling to badger me—"

"Chill, dill pickle," he interrupts. "I actually do care that you arrived there safely. But yes, I am looking forward to the day you point that Range Rover back in this direction."

"You need to forget I was ever your client. That would make all of this easier for you."

"I have three new offers on my desk for you. Two that came in yesterday. And one this morning. Should I just ignore them?"

"I'm not taking on new projects. I don't want to fire you as my agent, but I might have to for you to believe me."

"Ouch. That smarts."

"It's not personal. You know that. This is about my life. I'm at a crossroads, Joseph. In the past, I've driven straight through without considering what other directions I could take. I'm not going to do that this time."

"Not even if there's another hit series at the end of the straight road?"

I laugh. I can't help it. "You're incorrigible."

"That's what my mother always said."

"She was right."

He sighs, and I can picture him leaning back in his chair, feet on his big walnut desk, the L.A. cityscape his view. "I wish you would tell me what happened, Keegan. I might have been able to help."

"It wasn't anything that you or anyone else could help me with, Joseph. I'm in a place I arrived at all on my own."

"You sound like you think you've done something terrible," he says.

I hesitate, and then, "I didn't mean to."

"And I'm sure you didn't."

"I've spent the entirety of my children's lives working, trying to reach the next rung on the ladder. And now I have two children who basically can't stand to be around me."

"Keegan, that's not you. It's their age. All teenagers hate their parents."

"I don't believe that. When I was their age, all I wanted was parents who loved me and to be a part of a family."

"Okay, so they're rotten. They don't appreciate you. Or all that you've done for them. One day they will."

"I'm not so sure about that," I say. "Reece . . . she feels lost to me. I couldn't let the same thing happen with Evan."

"I get it," Joseph says. "I just wish you would leave some doors open."

"I'm afraid if I do, I'll come back. I don't want to be locked into the fear I've always let drive me. Fear that if I don't take every opportunity, there won't be another one. I've lived with that as my lighthouse for long enough. I don't want to live like that anymore."

"Do you know how many people would love to have the opportunities you've had, Keegan?"

There's a slight edge in his voice now, and I know that he will never understand why I've walked away. But, in all fairness, I haven't told him the whole truth so I really shouldn't be surprised. "I think I do, Joseph. But you know those opportunities came with a lot of sacrifice. Some of which I already regret."

I hear Evan tromp down the stairs and head out the front door without saying anything.

"I better go," I say. "Thanks for checking in."
"Sure you don't want to hear about just one offer—"
"Bye, Joseph," I say and end the call.

*

That which is not good for the bee-hive cannot be good for the bees.

– Marcus Aurelius

Bowie

THE SUN IS setting, shadows starting to fall across the lake side of the house when Carson and I head back up from the dock. We took the boat out in the late afternoon and idled around for a while. I admit I did ride by the Monroe house, telling myself I just wanted to see what it looked like in daylight. But when I thought I caught a glimpse of Keegan through one of the big glass windows, I slammed the accelerator forward so fast that it nearly knocked Carson out of the boat. He'd given me a severe look of disapproval before returning to his position at the bow, ears flying out to the side, tongue lolling.

He would be right to criticize me for my lapse. I don't have any idea what I was thinking to drive by her house like some infatuated fan.

Maybe it's been too long since I had a date. Maybe I need to work on that.

Carson barks and takes off across the grass. Keegan Monroe's son is walking toward us in running shorts and a soaked-with-sweat T-shirt.

"Hey, Mr. Dare," he calls out, stopping to squat down and rub Carson, who is now giving him a full body-wag welcome.

"Hey, Evan. Don't let him lick you to death."

"I like it," Evan says, and, of course, that makes me like him more.

"Out for a run?"

"Yeah. It's hotter than I thought."

"The humidity is what gets you."

"Yeah," he says, wiping his face with his shirt. "Another thing to love about Virginia."

Not sure how to respond to that, I say, "Can I get you something to drink?"

"Some water would be great."

I wave him toward the porch. "Come on in."

We go inside, and while I put ice in glasses, Carson drinks half of his water bowl, lapping loudly.

"He's such a cool dog," Evan says, and I hear some envy in his voice.

"He's my buddy," I say.

"So are you just here for the summer or what?" he asks, sitting down on one of the kitchen barstools.

"No. We live here full time."

"You don't get bored?"

"Haven't so far."

"How do you even meet people in a place like this?"

I smile, shake my head a little. It's clear he thinks his mother has moved him to the North Pole minus the ice caps. "Sports teams. There's a popular youth group at the Baptist church."

"Oh." His response is released with the same weight as a car with a suddenly flat tire.

"I've also seen a group of kids over at the marina who are part of the waterskiing club."

"I don't water-ski."

"Ah."

"Sorry, I'm not trying to be difficult. I'm just a little bummed about this whole move."

"At your age," I say, "I guess it would be kind of hard. Leaving your friends and all that."

"Yeah, it was."

I get the feeling he wants to tell me why. But I don't ask because it's not really any of my business. And I'm not sure I should be a sounding board for resentment against his mom's decision to move them across the country.

"What do you do here?" he asks, his tone implying there's no answer that could possibly make sense to him.

"I write books," I say.

He raises an eyebrow, as if I've surprised him. "Cool. About what?"

"Thriller-type stuff."

"I'll look you up."

"Do you like to read?"

"Yeah, I do, actually. A lot."

"What kind of stuff?"

"Sci-fi. Just read a book called *The Martian*. This guy gets left on Mars during a duststorm and has to figure out how to survive. It was pretty believable."

"That's the best kind of fiction. When you believe it could happen but wouldn't actually want to go through it yourself."

"Yeah, I think so too. So what did you do before you moved here and became a writer?"

"I've always written. Since I was twelve. I wanted to write a book that made somebody else feel like the ones I loved made me feel. Somewhere along the way I took a detour and worked for the FBI."

"Really?" Now I've really surprised him. "Doing what?"

"Stuff I'm not allowed to tell you about." I can see by the

look on his face I've gone up several notches in his estimation.

"But you write about it?"

"On some level, I guess we have to write about what we know."

"Now I have to read your books. Why did you leave your job with the FBI?"

"It was time." I realize that explains absolutely nothing to him, but it really mostly covers it all.

"Did you work a desk job?"

"I mostly worked drug-related cases."

"Wow. I bet you do have a lot to write about."

I notice then that Carson isn't on the porch. I step out into the yard and call him. When he doesn't answer after a couple of tries, I get concerned and tell Evan, "I'll be right back. I think he's asleep down at the dock or something."

"I'll come with you," Evan says.

We walk across the yard, and all the while I'm still calling. Just before we get to the dock, I see Carson's nose sticking out from under the bottom branches of a holly bush.

Frowning, I squat down and call him again, but he won't come. He barks a couple of times as if warning me about something. And it's only then that I notice the bees flying low to the ground just in front of us.

"Yellow jackets!" I shout. "Run, Evan! Back to the house!"

"Ow!" he yells, slapping at his leg.

"Run!"

He does, and I try to cut around the bees to get to Carson. He's still hunkered under the bush, and now I understand why. "Come on, boy!" I say. But he's not budging.

He whimpers. I squat down in front of the bush, feeling the bees landing on my jeans, and then stinging around my ankles. I reach under the limbs, pulling Carson out against his will. I scoop him up in my arms, no small feat considering his weight and resistance, and then take off running through the yard to the house.

"Evan!" I call out. There's no answer, and I don't see him.

I leap onto the porch, still carrying Carson as I shoulder open the door that leads to the living room. I set him down and slam the door closed with my foot at the same time. His tail wags full force, and he tries to lick my face in gratitude.

"You're okay, boy," I say. "Let me take a look at you."

I rub my hands across his fur, pulling it back to see if he has any stings. Miraculously, I don't see anything. The thickness of his coat most likely kept him from getting stung. And the bush, of course.

I stand up, calling for Evan again. When there's no answer, I run to the kitchen. "Evan?"

Just inside the doorway, I see him lying on the floor, face down.

"Evan," I say, dropping to my knees beside him. I place a hand on his back, shaking him gently. But there's no response, and that's when I notice his swelling face.

The bees.

He must be having a reaction.

I continue calling his name as my mind races for what to do. Benadryl. No. This looks as if it's already beyond that.

And then I remember the EpiPen in my medicine cabinet.

A couple of years ago, I started having reactions to foods that had never bothered me before, and my doctor prescribed the EpiPen as a just-in-case measure. I bolt to my feet to get it, then remember Evan's mom, and reach for his phone on the floor beside him. I run upstairs to my bedroom, scrolling his recent calls as I go, until I see Mom. I hit call with the phone to my ear as I open the bathroom cabinet, reaching for the EpiPen kit in the back.

"Hey, Ev," Keegan answers. "Where are you?"

"Ah, Keegan, Ms. Monroe, this is Bowie Dare," I say, trying to keep my voice calm. "Evan came over to my house, and while he was here, he was stung by a bee. Maybe several. He's having a reaction. I have an EpiPen here. I think he needs it."

"What?"

"He's having a reaction to bee stings—"

"Oh, no," she says then, as if my words are just breaking through her disbelief. "Yes, please! Please help him! I'm on the way!"

She clicks off then, and I head for the stairs, dialing 911 as I go.

*

Signs may be but the sympathies of nature with man.
— Charlotte Brontë, *Jane Eyre*

Keegan

I RACE OUT of the house and jump in the Rover, praying as hard as I know how. I floor the accelerator down the two-lane road that leads to Bowie Dare's house, my heart beating so hard I feel sick.

My mind is racing with potential scenarios. What if the EpiPen doesn't work? He's never had a reaction to anything before.

But then I already know that life can change in an instant. I've learned that with one child. *Dear God, please don't take this one from me too.*

I remember the turnoff we took when we stopped to ask directions and spit gravel down the long driveway, slamming to a crooked stop in front of the house. I shove it in park and cut the engine. I jump out and run to the door, calling as I go, "Evan! Evan!"

"In here," Bowie answers.

I follow his voice and find him squatting beside my son who is lying on the floor. His eyes are open, but he looks dazed, stunned.

"Evan," I say, dropping to my knees beside him, my voice frantic. "Are you okay?"

He tries to say something, but the words don't come out.

"I think his throat is probably swollen," Bowie says. "I've called 911. They should be here any minute."

"Thank you," I say, hearing the gratitude in my voice. "For helping him so quickly and—"

"Of course," he says, putting a hand on my arm. "I'm just sorry it happened."

I glance at his hand, and he immediately jerks it away, as if he's just become aware of being too forward or stepping over a line.

I hear the siren from the ambulance, its wail bringing back the reality of what has happened. Evan tries to sit up, shaking his head.

"Hang on, buddy," Bowie says. "The EpiPen did its job, but it's a good idea to get the paramedics to check you out. You had a pretty severe reaction."

He drops back onto the floor, as if he doesn't have the energy to protest. I lace my hand through his and hold on tight. "It's going to be okay," I say. "You'll be fine, sweetie."

A loud knock sounds at the front door. Bowie jumps up to run and let them in. In seconds, two paramedics step into the kitchen. Their demeanor is one of calm, and I feel instantly grateful that they're here.

The young woman in a dark blue uniform looks at me and says, "Are you his mother?"

"Yes."

"Can you tell us what happened?"

I glance at Bowie who is standing just behind the paramedics. "He was stung by bees," Bowie says. "I'm not sure how many."

"What kind?" she asks, wrapping a blood-pressure cuff around Evan's arm as she talks.

"Yellow jackets, I'm pretty sure," he says.

"Has he ever had a reaction to bees before?" the other paramedic asks. He's quite a bit older, gray in his dark hair. His eyes are serious and focused as he inserts a needle for an IV in Evan's arm.

"No," I say. "He's never been allergic to anything."

"It happens like that sometimes," he says. "Lucky you had the EpiPen."

I look at Bowie and let him see my gratitude. Relief drains all the energy from my muscles, and I feel as if it is all I can do not to collapse in front of him. "Bowie is the one who saved him," I say. "Thank goodness—"

Bowie leans back and says, "You don't know how grateful I am that I had it here."

The woman paramedic places a piece of tape over the needle in Evan's arm and glances at us both. "You're his parents?"

"No," we say in unison, and then, I correct myself, "I mean I'm his mom. Evan was visiting here when he got stung."

"Okay," she says. "I think to be on the safe side we'll transport him to the emergency room and get him checked out. "Rocky Mount is a little closer so we'll take him there."

I nod and say, "May I ride with him?" But then I realize I won't have a car to get us home.

"I can follow so you'll have a ride back," Bowie says, as if he's read my mind.

We don't know anyone else here, and I have no idea if cabs exist in an area this small, so I say, "I hate to ask it of you, but I would really appreciate it."

"It's not a problem," he says.

The paramedics lift Evan onto a stretcher. Evan tries to protest, but his lips are swollen, and he's having trouble making the words come out.

"It's going to be all right, Ev," I say, clutching his hand between my own. But I have to let go as the paramedics start to roll him out of the house. And as I follow them, I have the horrible feeling that I have made a huge mistake in moving here. Uprooting Evan as if it is really possible to start over again. To at least get it right with him.

As signs go, it's not a good one.

Sometimes you find yourself in the middle of nowhere,
and sometimes in the middle of nowhere, you find yourself.
– Author Unknown

Bowie

I STAY CLOSE to the ambulance, or as close as I can without abusing the speed limit too badly. The lights are flashing and the siren sounds most of the way up Route 40 to Rocky Mount.

I left Carson at home, and for once, he didn't seem to mind, no doubt worn out by the bee scare.

I feel horrible about what's happened. Logically, I know it's not my fault. I didn't ask Evan to come over, but it did happen in my yard, and I do somehow feel responsible.

Maybe it was the look in Keegan Monroe's eyes when she saw her son lying on my kitchen floor. In my years with the FBI, I witnessed plenty of parental grief and loss. Drug overdoses have no mercy when it comes to that. But it had been more than unsettling to see untethered fear on her face.

At the ER, the ambulance pulls up to the patient entrance. I park in front of the hospital and go inside the admissions area where Keegan is already filling out paperwork. Should I call her Ms. Monroe? That seems weird.

I stand near the sitting area, looking at my phone for no other reason than I don't know what else to do with myself.

A woman seated a few feet away leans forward in her chair, lowering her reading glasses to focus on the admissions area.

"Isn't that the actress who plays on that show—" she breaks off, looking for the name. "*Aimless.*"

The woman sitting next to her is remarkably similar in appearance. Sisters? "In Rocky Mount? Right."

"You never know. And she looks just like her."

"So she has a twin," the other woman says.

"Is there ever a day," the first woman says, settling back into her chair and returning her attention to the book in her hand, "that you don't absolutely delight in being a party pooper?"

The second woman makes a sound of insulted disagreement and shakes her head. "You should just move on out to Hollywood where you can star-spot for real."

"Maybe I will."

"Good."

"Like you could live without me."

Definitely sisters, I decide.

Just then, Keegan looks up and waves me over. "Thank you so much for this," she says. "I don't know how long before he's released. I hate to ask you to wait around."

"I'm fine," I say. "I have my phone. I'll camp out in the waiting area and get an extra chapter written."

She looks surprised. "You're a writer?"

"Yeah," I say. "Headphones, and I can write anywhere."

"Okay. That's great. Thank you. Really."

I find a corner in the waiting area, away from the TV and the sisters and put in my noise-reducing earbuds. I read over what I wrote this morning, find the point in the story to pick up from, and I barely look up again for the next two hours.

Don't make assumptions.
– Miguel Ruiz

Keegan

HE'S THE ONLY ONE in the waiting area when I come back out. I walk over to his chair and say his name. "Bowie?"

I repeat it again before he looks up at me, his eyes a little glazed as if he's been somewhere else altogether. "Yeah?" he says, putting down his phone and standing.

"He's doing fine. They want to keep him overnight just for observation. Would you mind driving me back? I'll get my car and a few things for us both to stay the night."

"Sure," I say. "No problem."

"Okay," I say. "Ready if you are."

He follows me through the waiting area and out the main doors. The night air is instantly cool on my skin, and I welcome its freshness from the antiseptic smell of the hospital's interior.

Bowie hits the remote to the truck, and to my surprise, walks to the passenger side and opens the door for me. We meet eyes, and I see a flash of something like uncertainty that I will welcome the gesture. But it's charming and unexpected. "Thank you," I say, stepping up into the cab of the truck.

He shuts the door and walks around to the driver's side. The truck's interior is roomy, but as soon as he slides in,

I'm instantly aware of his sudden proximity and the pleasant tang of a masculine scent.

He reverses out of the lot and turns onto the street where we immediately have to stop for a red light. He glances at me and says, "I can't tell you how sorry I am about this."

"It's not your fault," I say. "It could have happened anywhere. And it could have happened with someone who didn't know what to do. Or have the medicine you had."

"Yeah," he says. "You don't know how thankful I am for that."

I think I can guess by the relief in his voice. It's not hard to understand the responsibility he would have felt. I glance out the passenger side window and sigh as we pass the beautiful white courthouse I remember seeing on the county website when I had been researching the area. "I'm wondering if this is a sign," I say, surprised that I've said the words out loud.

"What do you mean?" he asks, and I feel him glance over at me.

"I forced Evan to move here. He didn't want to."

"Kind of got that impression," he says. "My guess is it'll grow on him."

I look over at him and say, "I don't know. This might as well be another planet compared to L.A."

"True," he agrees. "But you must have seen something in it that felt right. I mean that's a pretty major move."

"I'm beginning to think it's not possible to find what I'm looking for," I say.

"What are you looking for?" he asks.

I glance off out the window again, my voice low enough that he might not hear me. "A second chance, I guess," I say.

But he has heard me because he says, "I have it on good authority that you can indeed find those here."

I turn my gaze on him again, but this time, he keeps his eyes straight ahead. I want to ask him what he means by that. But I somehow know that he wouldn't be any more anxious to share his secrets than I am to share mine.

In utter loneliness a writer tries to explain the inexplicable.
–John Steinbeck

Bowie

WE'RE BACK AT my house in under thirty minutes. I could have gotten her here a little faster, but I felt more inclined to stay with the speed limit because honestly, it felt nice to have her in the truck with me.

As I turn into the driveway, I remind myself that I need to start getting out a little more. Maybe actually asking someone out. I've avoided the thought of dating long enough that I'm only now just realizing my own loneliness.

I stop the truck just short of the house, turn off the engine and say, "I really hope he'll be fine by the time you get back to the hospital."

"Based on everything the doctors told me, I think he will," she says, not quite meeting my gaze.

"Would you mind calling and letting me know? I think I'll sleep better."

"Sure, what's your cell number?"

I give it to her, and she enters it in her phone. "All right, then," she says, opening the door. She starts to slide out, then turns back to me, as if she has decided to say something before changing her mind.

"Would you like to come over for dinner tomorrow night? Or tonight, actually," she corrects herself, glancing at her watch. "It's after midnight. So, can you come? As a thank you for everything—"

"You don't have to do that," I say. "I should be fixing you dinner as an apology."

"I'd like to," she says. "I'm a decent cook. I'll make it worth your while."

I shake my head a little, wondering if I've fallen asleep and am dreaming this conversation. Keegan Monroe wants to fix dinner for me. Is being rather insistent about it, in fact. I should wake up at any moment.

"Sure," I say, testing my theory.

"Great," she says, smiling, and either it's real, or the dream is continuing. "Six-thirty?"

"Six-thirty," I say. "You'll let me know about Evan?"

"I will," she says, starting to close the door, and then stopping. "Would you like to bring Carson?"

I'm pretty sure this is a stretch for her, and I appreciate it. "We'll see," I say, as I open my door. "Can I bring anything for the meal?"

"Just your appetite."

She walks to the Range Rover, hits the key remote to unlock it. Then she turns for a moment, lifts her hand and gets in the vehicle.

I watch her drive off, thinking life really is all kinds of strange. Of course, she's just being nice. Because she thinks she owes me. That's all the dinner is. To let myself start thinking there's anything other than that behind it would make me . . . naive at best.

That's not a word that has ever applied to me in any other capacity.

I let Carson out and wait in the yard for him to do his business. I can tell he's still highly suspicious of the reappearance of bees. I don't blame him. Being chased by furious yellow jackets isn't something I care to repeat either.

He's glad I'm home because once we're back in the house, he sticks close, following me from the living room to kitchen where I grab a bottle of water and drink half of it before sticking it back in the fridge.

The clock above the sink indicates it's well past my bedtime, but I'm not in the least bit sleepy. I don't feel like writing either. Without giving myself time to question the wisdom of it, I pick up the TV remote and flick on the screen. I find the smaller remote and turn on Apple TV, scroll down until I find Netflix. I search the listings for the show. There. *Aimless*. Season One. Episode One.

I sit down on the couch, and Carson jumps up beside me, putting his head on my leg and dropping off to sleep almost instantly. Me? I'm still awake at 4:30 when I click play for Episode Six.

*

You want your mom to be happy, but it can't be just any guy. Right? Right.
– Teenage Boys Everywhere

Evan

"I LOOK LIKE I'm trying to swallow a basketball."

Mom laughs, and I don't even blame her. I look that funny.

"It'll go away pretty quickly the doctor said," she says.

"It's the next morning, and I still look like this," I complain, even as I feel guilty for it. Honestly, I'm just happy to be alive.

"I, for one," she says, "am practicing gratitude."

"I know. Me too," I admit, taking a sip of the hospital's rather pitiful excuse for coffee. I don't think I'll even give the food a chance. The eggs look like a plastic imitation of eggs.

"I invited Mr. Dare over for dinner tonight," she says, busying herself with fixing my blanket. "As a thank you."

"Oh. Yeah. I'll call him on the drive home."

"He might have saved your life," she says.

"He probably did. But you don't need to use that as an excuse for inviting him to dinner."

She leans back and looks at me with widened eyes. "Evan."

"What? I saw the way you looked at him. The way he looked at you."

"He did not—"

"Mom. How many times do you think I've seen men look at you like that? I mean, at least he curbed the lust."

"Evan Monroe."

"Sorry. Most of them don't."

She starts to say something, but stops, and a look crosses her face that I've seen a lot in the past few months. Like she's realized, really realized, she's failed as a mother. I instantly regret being the one to bring the realization to the surface again. Even if it's not something I agree with.

"It just blows to see someone look at your mom like that."

"I could wear a bag over my head," she says, regaining her sense of humor.

"I'm not sure it would help. They'd just look at—"

"Evan," she says, her voice sharpening.

"Okay, okay," I say.

"Despite the basketball cheeks, I think you're ready to go home," she says.

"Hey," I say. "Not fair."

"Turnabout is fair play," she says, giving me the eye that means she's one-upped me.

"How long before I can get out of here and get some real food?"

*

No man is an island, entire of itself; every man is a piece of the continent, a part of the main.

–John Donne

Keegan

REAL FOOD IS a stop at the Rocky Mount McDonald's drive-through. Evan won't hear of going in with his face still swollen, so I order enough for three men and drive toward the lake while he eats.

I honestly do not know where he puts it, but he's six-two and hasn't quit growing yet.

We're only a few miles from the house when I spot a white tent off the right-hand side of the road and a red sign that says FRESH VEGGIES in white lettering. I flip the turn signal and swing in, parking beside a white Denali with a magnetic sign on the door that says "Hayden's Marina – Gas, Picnic Supplies and Fine Dining."

"I'm staying in the car," Evan says, as if I've just pulled up to a science fair, and he'll be forced to attend a lecture on atoms.

I decide I'm going to enjoy the stop anyway. I get out and walk to the white tent fifteen or so yards away where a beautiful spread of produce has been artfully arranged on long wooden tables.

A woman stands in front of one, examining the tomatoes. Another woman is working behind the tables, sorting through yellow squash. She's dressed in a long dress with a cape around the shoulders. Her hair is covered by a white bonnet. I recognize the dress as belonging to the German Baptist community of Franklin County.

The woman looks up and throws me a welcoming smile, her face devoid of makeup. She is refreshingly pretty, and I find myself giving her back a genuine smile.

"Let me know if you see anything I can help you with. The potatoes are fresh out of the garden. Actually, everything you see on the tables will be from our own gardens, except for the tomatoes. These are coming out of South Carolina."

"Thank you," I say, reaching for a brown paper bag and picking up a cucumber.

"They're still beautiful," the woman a few feet away says, holding up a tomato. "Yours will be better, Mary, but these should pass Kat's inspection."

"What did she and Myrtle whip up for your lunch crowd today?" the woman named Mary asks.

"When I left this morning, Myrtle was working on black-eyed peas and cornbread. I think Kat was making gnocchi with fresh tomato sauce. So we'll need some more," she says, holding up a big red tomato.

"Those two are some kind of cooks," Mary says.

"They keep each other entertained," the woman says. "I know Kat's looking forward to having a little brother."

The woman places a hand on her stomach, and I see then that she's pregnant. "Congratulations," I say, smiling as we meet gazes.

"Thank you," she says, her eyes all but glowing with happiness.

"When are you due?" I ask.

"Before Christmas," she says. She tips her head to the right and looks at me for a long moment. "Have we met?"

Before I can answer, she says, "Oh, you're . . . you play on that show . . . *Aimless?*"

"I did," I say. "My son Evan and I just moved here."

"That's wonderful," she says, sticking out her hand. "I'm Gabby Tatum."

"Keegan Monroe," I say, not wanting to assume she knows my name.

"Yes," she says. "You were what made that series so interesting. I really enjoyed it."

"Thank you," I say, forcing myself to accept the compliment without negating it.

"My family and I run the marina down the road," she says. "You should stop by when you're out on the lake."

"We will," I say.

"Mom?"

I turn to see Evan with his head sticking out the window of the Rover. "Yes?"

"Your phone is ringing. It's Bowie Dare. Want me to answer?"

"Sure," I say. He ducks back in the vehicle, my phone to his ear.

When I look back at Gabby Tatum, she's assessing me with a soft smile. "You've already attracted the interest of our mysterious Mr. Dare?" she says, a note of teasing in her voice.

"Oh, no," I say. "Not like that. My son stopped at his house late yesterday and got into a yellow jacket's nest. He had a pretty severe reaction. Mr. Dare—I mean, Bowie, was able to treat him with an EpiPen—"

"Oh, goodness," she says. "I'm sorry. That's so scary."

"It was," I say. "He's never reacted to anything before."

"I'm glad he's okay," she says, her expression reflecting concern.

"Me too," I agree. I know I'll be adding fuel to the fire, but can't resist asking, "Why mysterious?"

"Mr. Dare?"

"Yes."

She smiles. "Given how he looks, half the county's single women have tried to snag his interest. No telling how many coconut-cream pies the man has had left on his doorstep."

"Ah. Hope he likes coconut."

We both laugh.

"To my knowledge, none of them has actually worked yet. I do see him in town with his dog, and at the marina occasionally too."

"You don't think he's married or anything, do you?"

"Rumor has it he isn't. But you can't really rely on rumors around here," she says with a smile. "The grapevine can get a little tangled."

"Yeah. I don't think small towns have a corner on that."

"Were you in L.A. or New York?"

"L.A."

"I guess you're expecting some culture shock," she says.

"Maybe a little. But I think I'm ready for it. A quieter pace, I mean."

"Ummm," she says, and I can tell she's wondering if I truly understand the difference between there and here.

"Well, if anyone can turn our intriguing Mr. Dare's head, it will be you," she says. "My gosh, you're beautiful. I love being pregnant, but I already feel like I'm being slowly inflated every day."

I laugh. "You're gorgeous. You have that glow that only pregnant women who are very loved have."

"Thank you," she says. "I am that. And so grateful for it."

I have the feeling that if we knew each other a bit better,

she would elaborate on what she means. I decide that I like her and realize how long it's been since I've had a real friend.

"We're supposed to have our boat in a couple of days," I say. "We'll come by the marina. I hope you're there."

"Me too," she says. "I'd love to introduce you to my husband and daughter."

"I'll look forward to it."

"Great," she says, handing her bag to Mary who rings up her purchase and takes her money.

She steps back from the table then and smiles at me, before saying, "And I'll look forward to hearing about your dinner with Mr. Dare."

She's teasing me again, but I don't mind. It's kind of nice to be talking with a woman who isn't sizing me up to see how we compare as competition for a role or a man.

I hand my produce to Mary, and she starts ringing it up, waving as Gabby Tatum backs out and pulls off.

"She's so nice," I say, looking at Mary.

"She is," Mary agrees. "Been through some rough patches lately, so it's nice to see that."

I'm not normally prone to curiosity about people's personal lives, but I find myself wondering what kind of rough patches. I don't ask though, and Mary doesn't elaborate.

She bags my produce, thanks me for my business, and says, "Hope you'll come back soon."

"I will," I say. "I like to cook. Fresh always makes it better."

I'm back in the car when Evan asks, "Why is she dressed so funny?"

"Evan," I admonish, pulling back onto the main road. "It's part of her belief system. There's a German Baptist community here that practices living in a non-showy way."

"It would be hard to have to dress like that every day."

"Not if you were raised that way, and it was what you were used to."

"I'm glad I wasn't raised like that," he says, his tone indicating it would have been the worst thing ever.

"It's okay for people to be different, Evan. To live differently."

"Oh, like you would be happy to wear a long dress and a bonnet every day?" he scoffs.

"She looked happy, Ev. As if she likes her life. More and more, I'm beginning to think that's all that matters."

"Who are you, and what did you do with my mom?"

I shake my head and smile a little. "I'm the mom who chased a dream at the expense of all else."

"That's not true," he says, his voice softening. "No matter what Reece has said to you, you've given us a good life, Mom. A great life. Maybe we could have seen you a little more, but hey, you don't have to be a bona fide adult to realize life is about choices and compromises. We don't get to have it all."

"How old are you?" I ask him, feeling a surge of love for his unexpected empathy.

"Old enough to know."

I reach across and put my hand over his. And for the first time in a long while, he doesn't pull away.

*

I care not for a man's religion whose dog and cat are not the better for it.

— Abraham Lincoln

Bowie

IT'S RIDICULOUS. I never care about what I wear. I buy clothes that make sense for whatever it is I'm going to be wearing them for. And pull them out of my closet based on practicality.

So why am I standing here staring at my row of shirts as if I've never seen any of them before?

It's a thank-you dinner. That is all. It doesn't matter what I look like.

Carson rolls over on my bed, sticking his paws up in the air and letting out a long sigh. Apparently, he's gotten bored with my debate.

I force myself to grab a pair of jeans and a dark gray polo-type shirt. It doesn't take a genius to realize how many guys she must be constantly turning down. Do I really want to get in that line-up?

No. If I took anything away from my marriage to Erin, it is that you shouldn't ignore the little voice that warns you when something is a stretch. No doubt the voice warned me. No doubt I ignored it.

The voice warning me this time is blaring at megaphone volume. I shrug into the shirt, wondering if I should back out of going altogether. She probably just felt obligated to do something nice for me because of Evan. Of course, she did. But wouldn't it be rude to cancel a half hour before I'm supposed to be there?

Yes, it would.

Okay, so I'm going.

"You're going too, Carson. Come on, let's go get your fancy collar on."

He hops off the bed and follows me out of the room, tail wagging.

I PULL INTO the driveway and park behind Keegan's Range Rover.

I feel like a sixteen year old, picking up a girl for a first date. I know how ridiculous this is and all the reasons why it's not even accurate. I'm not here for a date. And I'm not sixteen.

I take a deep breath and slide out of the truck, waiting for Carson to hop out. The front door of the house opens, and Evan appears, hands in the pockets of his jeans.

"Hey, Mr. Dare," he says.

"Bowie's good," I say. "How are you feeling?"

"Much better," he says. "I'm glad to be off the might-be-kin-to-a-chipmunk list."

I smile and say, "I believe the nurses were still checking you out."

He shoves his hands in his pockets and looks embarrassed. "Nah. Come on in," he adds, leaning down to rub Carson under the chin. "I should have hidden under the bush with you, huh?"

Evan leads us into the kitchen where Keegan is putting salad ingredients into a large stainless-steel bowl. She looks up and smiles at me. "Hey," she says.

"Hey," I throw back, keeping my tone neutral in defiance of my leaping stomach.

I try not to notice, but she looks incredible. Her blonde hair is pulled back in a loose ponytail. She's wearing a white tank top, designer-looking jeans, and she's barefoot.

I am so glad I didn't go the dressed-up route and ended up looking like I was trying way too hard.

"Would you like a glass of wine?" she asks. "We have red and white."

"Red would be good," I say.

Carson walks over to her and sits at her side, looking up in clear anticipation of her attention. She looks down at him, attempts to pet his head, but quickly pulls her hand back, before she says, "Should I put a bowl of water down for him?"

"He's fine," I say.

Carson throws me a questioning glance, as if he's not sure what to do next. He isn't used to being rejected by humans. I feel bad for him, but I'm almost glad to find a reason not to be attracted to her. I could never fall for a woman who didn't like my dog. So there you have it. No need for the butterflies. Or the agonizing over the wardrobe. I'll eat the dinner she's prepared and then we'll be on our way.

Except that it doesn't go exactly like that.

When we sit down at the rectangular table in her dining room, she passes me a small plate, featuring bite-size pieces of the roasted chicken she has prepared, a mound of green peas, and three baby carrots.

"Can you give that to Carson? I hope he likes those things. I wasn't sure."

Carson is sitting by my chair, and at the sound of his name, wags his tail expectantly. It makes a swish-swish sound on the hardwood floor. "Sure," I say, taking the plate from her, even as I realize that my plan to actively dislike her has now been decimated by an act of kindness that a true dog-hater would never be able to fake.

Carson tucks into the food as if he hasn't eaten in a week.

"Thank you," I say. "That was really nice."

"He likes your cooking, Mom," Evan says.

"Great," she says. "Let's see if you two agree with him."

THE FOOD IS amazing. At one point, I can't help asking her, "Did you go to culinary school or something?"

"No," she says, shaking her head and looking pleased by the question. "I just love food and started reading a lot of books on how to prepare it. It's become a hobby, I guess."

"Lucky for Evan," I say.

Evan shrugs and says, "She gets a little fancy sometimes."

"I try to keep it in line with the teenage palette."

Despite his assessment of Keegan's cooking, he cleans his

plate while we're still eating. He pushes back his chair and says, "All right if I go up and Skype a friend, Mom?"

She looks startled by the question, as if she hadn't planned on being left alone with me. But I suppose there's no graceful way to make him stay at the table, because she says, "Okay. Keep it PG."

"Mom."

"Evan."

"Can Carson come up with me, Bowie?" he asks.

"Sure," I say.

Evan calls him, and Carson takes off up the stairs right behind him.

The silence in the room following their departure is awkward to say the least. We both start to speak at the same time, stop, and then I say, "Go ahead."

"I was just going to say I sometimes wish all this computer communication stuff had never been invented."

"I would think it makes parenting a lot harder."

"You really can't imagine all the things they can get into. I mean you try to foresee it, put rules in place. But the temptation is just too much for them to resist."

"It's hard for a lot of adults to resist," I say. "I was watching this documentary the other night where a woman pretended to be her eighteen-year-old daughter online. She went into chat rooms and developed relationships with guys. One of them ended up shooting another one over her. It was only afterward that they found out she was a forty-seven-year-old mother."

Keegan leans back, her eyes wide. "Seriously?"

"Yeah," I say.

"That's so beyond crazy. How could a mother do that to her daughter?"

"Anonymity prods people to do things they wouldn't do in plain sight. The internet provides that. You can be whomever your picture says you are."

She takes a sip of her wine and says, "You must have seen some difficult-to-believe stuff in your line of work. Evan mentioned you worked for the FBI at one time."

"The worst and the best," I say.

"Did it change how you see people?"

"I'd like to say no. That the bad people don't get to do that to us. But it takes its toll after a while. I guess evil is like weeds. You think you've pulled it up by the roots, that it's gone for good. And then there it is again. As if your previous efforts had done nothing at all."

Her expression has a hint of caught-in-the-headlights. I instantly apologize.

"You certainly didn't ask for that much information, did you?"

She shakes her head a little. "It's okay. Actually, I think most of us walk around with our head in the clouds, oblivious to just how much bad there is out there."

"It's not such a bad place to be. Oblivion."

"Do you write about all of this?" she asks. "The things you know about humanity now?"

I shrug, swirling my wine in the glass. "Some of it. Not all of it. My feeling is that people read to escape. I try to remember that when I'm walking that line between entertaining and venting my views on the world."

"I'd like to read one of your books. Which one should I start with?"

"You don't have to do that," I say, assuming she's just being polite.

"I love to read. Give me a title."

I do so, reluctantly. Why, I'm not sure. Is it because I don't want to be judged against her creative standards? Or because I'm not comfortable with her looking for pieces of me based on what we've been talking about?

She picks up her phone from its place on the table, taps the screen, taps a few more times, and then says, "There. I'll start it tonight before bed."

"Thanks," I say. And then for distraction, "The meal was incredible. Can I help you clear up?"

"I'll get it later. How about some coffee on the deck?'

"Sounds great," I say.

"Head on out. I'll get everything together and meet you there."

I start to insist on helping, but decide to do as she suggested. Outside, the night air is a welcome relief to the heat in my face. I don't normally find it that easy to talk to a woman I barely know. I guess I'm out of practice. But something about Keegan makes it easy. Her seemingly genuine interest.

I remember for a moment the last couple years of my marriage and how Erin and I had gotten to the point where we really never talked. Two people living under the same roof, and little more.

The French door to the deck opens, and Keegan walks through with a tray. A French press pot, two white cups, and cream and sugar containers sit in the middle.

"I can take that," I say, walking over to get it.

"You can just put it on the table," she says.

I do, and she pours me a cup before handing it to me and saying, "Fix it the way you like it?"

"Black is good," I say, taking a sip. "Um, good coffee."

"It's one of my weaknesses. That's an Italian blend. Little hard to find, but my favorite."

She adds some cream to hers and then goes over to the rail, leaning forward to look out at the night-darkened lake. "It's unbelievably peaceful here," she says.

"It is," I agree, walking over to lean on the railing but being careful to leave a few feet between us. "I'm not sure I could ever get used to the constant sound of traffic again."

"D.C.?"

I nod.

"Do people there consider horn-blowing a natural-born right?"

I smile. "It's one of those things I never got used to. It's like constantly be yelled at."

"I know," she says. "And, of course, there's the old stand-by middle finger."

"I guess driving in big cities isn't for the faint of heart."

"Definitely not."

We sip in silence for a minute or more, and then I say, "I guess I should be going. The dinner was amazing."

"Oh," she says, sounding disappointed. "Can you stay a little longer?"

The question surprises me, but I say, "Maybe I'll have one more cup of coffee."

She takes my cup and refills it from the pot on the table, then walks back over and hands it to me.

"Did you ever look for missing people when you were with the FBI?"

I look at her over the rim of my cup, raising an eyebrow. "Ah, yes. Fairly often, actually."

"May I ask you something?"

"Sure."

"How do you find someone who doesn't want to be found?"

"It's not easy. But people leave a lot of footprints today that they aren't always aware of."

"Oh," she says, looking down at her cup. And then, "It's my daughter. I haven't seen her in almost a year."

"I'm sorry," I say. "Is she a runaway?"

"She's nineteen, so I guess technically, no."

"That makes it a lot harder then."

"She can go where she wants, right?"

"Right."

"I just wish I could know she's okay. That would make it all so much more bearable."

I'm not exactly sure what to say. I wonder then if this is why I was asked over tonight. "Do you think she's in L.A.?" I ask.

"I'm assuming so. Although no one we know has seen her. Or at least admitted to it, anyway."

"And you know she's—"

"Alive?"

I nod because it seems like saying it out loud might cause her pain.

"Yes. She told Evan that she didn't want me to try to find her. That's how much she hated her life I guess."

"I'm sorry. I can't begin to imagine how painful that must be."

She takes another sip of her coffee and stares out into the darkness. "You think you know someone. Your own child, anyway. For most of her life, I think I have known her. But something changed in her. She didn't want to tell me things anymore. I thought it was just normal for a teenager to do that. Part of the pulling away and developing wings stage.

And so I never really questioned her about it. I thought with time, things would get back to being like they once were between us. But they didn't."

"Did she go to college?"

Keegan shakes her head. "She had planned to, and then a month before it was time to leave, she decided she didn't want to. A few weeks later, she told me she was pregnant and that she was having an abortion. I was heartbroken. I just couldn't believe she would do that. I even told her I would raise the child, but she wouldn't agree. That's when she left, and I haven't seen her since."

I try to think of something to say. But I can't find any words that seem up to the task of comforting her. I finally manage a lame-sounding, "That must have been difficult for you."

"It was. Is. I almost made the same choice myself. With Reece. Now, I don't know how I could ever have considered that. To think that Reece might not have been born—"

She breaks off there, turns to look at me and says, "I have no idea why I'm telling you all of this. I don't make a habit of opening up my closet of personal stuff and forcing it on others."

"I don't mind," I say, realizing that I really don't. It's been a long time since I've had a personal conversation with anyone. Most of the people I've met here are acquaintances, and we don't get past the small talk phase. But then I'm good at keeping people in that particular phase. Which makes me wonder why I haven't sought a way out of this very personal conversation.

"Do you have children?" she asks, looking directly at me.

"No," I say. "My wife, ex-wife, and I were pretty focused on careers. She's an attorney and didn't see herself becoming a mother."

"Do you regret not having them?"

"Sometimes," I admit.

"It's not too late," she says. "You're young."

I shrug and say, "I think I probably missed that milestone."

"I have to say it's been the most rewarding part of my life and the most difficult."

"Even compared to a career in acting?"

"Even compared to that," she says, smiling a little. "It's a slippery slope. I thought I was doing a good job at juggling being a single parent and having a career, but I was wrong."

"No one gets it perfect," I say.

"I agree with that. But I'm beginning to wonder if you really can't do both."

"Sometimes, people don't have a choice. Did you?"

She shakes her head. "Not for a long time anyway. I was on welfare until Reece was five and Evan four. I would take whatever job I could get, waitressing and auditioning for commercials, bit parts for TV shows. It took five years of that kind of work before I landed anything significant and could stop the waitressing."

"That must have been hard."

She shrugs. "I wanted to give them the life I never had growing up. To really make it so they would never want for anything. I thought it was worth every moment of discomfort, every rejection, because I was doing it for my children."

"Do you regret any of it?"

"I think I should have spent more time with them. That it would have mattered more in the long run than being able to give them the latest and greatest."

"You know I don't have the insight of having been a

parent, but if you did what you did for them out of love, I don't think you should be so hard on yourself."

"We just don't get a do-over, you know?"

I put my forearms on the railing, leaning forward without meeting her gaze. "Unfortunately, that's true for most things in life."

"Anything in particular you're talking about?"

"Work, I guess. What I chose to do for a career."

"Do you regret it?"

"Parts of it."

"Why?"

I don't answer for several seconds because it's hard to know what to say. I finally just admit, "Because on some days I wish I could go back to believing that people are basically good and the world is an okay place."

"You saw a lot of bad stuff," she says, the words a statement instead of a question.

"Yeah," I say.

"How did you deal with it?"

"You have to develop a way to close it off in your mind when it's time to be a regular person. I was able to do that for a long time. But the bad began to seep through my wall, and I wasn't able to keep my work life separate from my personal life any longer."

"Is that what happened to your marriage?"

"I'm sure it didn't help it."

Keegan looks at me for several moments before saying, "It's good to feel things for others. You shouldn't belittle yourself for that."

"Yeah. It was just the signal that told me it was time for a change."

"I've always thought it would be awesome to be able to write. When did you start?"

"I've kept journals since I was a teenager, but I started writing novels a few years before I left the bureau. It was a way for me to make the bad guys do what I wanted them to do."

She laughs. "Well, apparently a lot of people enjoy what you make them do. I'm looking forward to reading your work."

"Keegan, you really don't have to—"

"I want to," she interrupts. "Does it make you uncomfortable when people you know read your books?"

I start to deny it, but stop myself. "A little."

"I'm the same with the acting I've done. I'd far rather think of strangers watching me than friends."

"Weird, isn't it?"

She nods. "Just so you know, I'm not in the habit of opening up a vein the way I've done with you tonight. I'm sorry if I unloaded too much."

"You didn't," I say. "I've enjoyed our conversation." And since it seems like it might be time to do so, I add, "I should be going."

"Thanks for coming over, Bowie. And again, for what you did for Evan."

"And thank you for the amazing dinner. Haven't eaten that well in a long time. You sure I can't help you clean up?"

"Positive," she says.

We snag gazes for a moment, the light from the half-moon providing the only relief from the dark. I can't think of another word to say because all I can do is look at her. I find her beautiful. I can't deny that. But there's something else too that draws me to her. Maybe it's her honesty and the revelations that make her more human than most people I've met. Even with her enviable Hollywood life, she is very real and down to earth.

I guess this has surprised me.

I'm overcome with the desire to put my hand to the side of her face, rub my thumb across her full lower lip. I see in her eyes that she knows I want to touch her. She doesn't step back, and although this isn't an invitation, I know it isn't rejection either.

"Mom?"

Evan's voice calls out from the kitchen, muted through the French doors. The handle turns and Evan and Carson walk out onto the deck. Carson trots over to give me a sniff, as if he needs to make sure I'm still out here.

"Finished with your call?" Keegan asks.

"Yeah," Evan says. "This long-distance stuff isn't going to work. She's already talking to other guys."

"If she is," Keegan says, "that will prove she wasn't the right one for you."

"So now I'm not only a hostage but a monk as well?"

"Evan—" she begins.

"Chill, Mom," he says. "We're cool."

"We should be going," I say, reaching down to rub Carson's head. "Thank you again for the dinner."

"'Bye, Mr. Dare—I mean, Bowie," Evan says.

"See ya', Evan. Goodnight, Keegan," I add, not meeting eyes with her again as Carson and I head for the truck.

*

I want to live my life so that my nights are not full of regrets.

– D. H. Lawrence

Keegan

I CAN'T SLEEP.

It's not for lack of trying. I toss and turn until almost three before giving up. I turn on the lamp and reach for my laptop, opening the lid with a yawn.

I feel physically fatigued, but my brain is wide-open, refusing to shut down.

Maybe I shouldn't have talked about Reece with Bowie tonight. Doing so has filled me with renewed longing to find her.

For the past couple of months, I have forced myself to stop the daily rituals of haunting her Facebook page, tapping into her Instagram account, checking to see if she's been on Twitter.

I started to feel like a stalker, obsessed with any possible detail of her whereabouts. For my own sanity, I stopped because she never posted on any of the accounts anyway, unwilling to provide me with clues that might give away her location.

But tonight, I'm filled with renewed determination to find her. With the pain of this past year, I really have no choice but to accept that she wants to live her life apart from me. I just need to know she's okay.

I search her name in every social media outlet I can think of. Where I find an account for her, there are no new posts for nearly a year. This worries me as much as anything because Reece lived for social media, never went anywhere without her phone in her hand. The phone I got for her, the one that is still on my account, hasn't been turned on for just as long.

If it weren't for the email she sent to Evan through a disposable email address, I would start to believe that she is no longer alive.

I slam the laptop shut and toss it to the other side of the bed.

I flick off the lamp and close my eyes against the darkness.

I truly hate being awake at this time of night, because I have no defenses against my own thoughts, my multitude of regrets.

The questions tap at my brain, relentless. How did I miss it? How could I not see the signs, the changes in her?

Was it that I hadn't wanted to? Or that I simply had not been around enough to put the pieces of the puzzle together?

I know the answer.

The TV series had reached a high point during Reece's senior year in high school. If I wasn't on the set filming a new episode, I was traveling somewhere for interviews, guest appearances.

My income was the highest it had ever been. I couldn't actually believe what they were willing to pay me per show. I had told myself it wouldn't be forever. And with the realities of an acting career, I knew I wasn't being unrealistic to think I might never have the same kind of opportunity again.

And so I made sacrifices in the amount of time I spent with

my children for the two years when I gave as much as I could to the role and helping the show to prosper.

I would give anything to do it all over again, knowing what I know now.

Except that isn't possible. Time is the one thing you can't get back.

I think about Bowie Dare then. The way he'd listened to me tonight. How easy he'd been to talk to.

Lying here now, I can't remember the last time I shared so much of my personal life with anyone. Somewhere along the way, I learned that some friends don't remain friends forever. And that tabloids love to find the people in your life who are willing to hand over personal details for the right amount of money.

So I stopped revealing too much of myself, until tonight with Bowie Dare. And I have no idea what makes him different.

But I sense that he is.

Maybe it's his eyes. It's as if he's seen things other people haven't seen. Wouldn't want to see. Whatever it is, he feels trustworthy. And maybe I just needed someone to talk to.

I think about that last look between us. The way his eyes had lingered on mine. The dip my stomach had taken. And I can't deny that I'm attracted to him. Smith Mountain Lake's "mysterious Mr. Dare."

But I need a friend way more than I need a boyfriend. Better to ignore that look altogether.

If I know anything, it is that relationships, at least the ones I've had, do not tend to last.

I came here to start fresh, create a new life. A person needs friends to do something like that.

So friends. It's what Bowie and I will be.

*

After all, a girl is – well, a girl. It's nice to be told you're successful at it.

– Rita Hayworth

Evan

IT'S AFTER TEN when I get up and go downstairs to find a note from Mom saying she's gone to the grocery store and will be back around lunchtime.

I open the refrigerator, stare at the leftovers from last night, a bowl of tomatoes and some yellow squash, before deciding to try out the marina down the road. Mom had said they have a cafe that's supposed to be good.

I take a quick shower and then get my bike out of the garage, heading down the driveway and then onto the two-lane road that leads to the marina. It's only a couple of miles away, and I cover the distance in ten minutes or so.

The sun is high and bright this morning, and I have to admit the scenery along the way is appealing in a way I'm not used to. Black cows graze the green pastures of small farms. A tractor with a mower on the back cuts the grass in a large field.

I take a left at the marina sign and follow a sloping driveway to the dock and cafe that sit on the waterfront.

I park my bike at the rear entrance, wondering if I should have brought along the chain to lock it up. But then I remember I'm not in L.A. anymore, and this doesn't look like the kind of place where a bike is likely to get stolen.

The marina is busy. Several vehicles are parked in the lot on the roadside of the building. I can see boats parked along the waterfront, a line of five or six idling in the cove while waiting for a spot to tie up.

I walk along the dock, stopping midway to watch a group of children feeding hundreds of carp fish from popcorn containers. One little boy is feeding them piece by piece, trying to aim the piece of popcorn perfectly at the round mouths sticking up out of the water. Another little girl dumps her entire container into the water, causing a feeding frenzy.

"Amazing, isn't it?"

I turn my head to find a pretty girl staring at me with a wide smile. She has a beautiful English accent, and I wonder what she's doing so far from home. "Yeah, I say. Can't say I've ever seen anything like it."

"Me either, the first time I saw them."

"Do they stay here all year or just in the summer?"

"We feed them all year, so even after the tourists leave at the end of the summer, they have no reason to go elsewhere to look for food."

"Cool," I say. I'm finding it hard to meet her gaze, but force myself to do so. Shyness isn't typical for me, but something about this girl makes me suddenly doubt my appeal to the opposite sex.

"I'm Analise," she says, sticking out her hand.

I stick mine out in return, noticing how petite her hand is. I raise my eyes to hers then, feeling a little jolt of something I've never felt before. "Evan," I say. "Nice to meet you."

"Nice to meet you," she says. "Are you here for the summer?"

"Ah, sort of," I say, not wanting to admit that we've moved here altogether because I'm still hoping it's temporary.

"Are you here to eat?"

"Yeah," I say. "Is breakfast over?"

"Not if we ask Myrtle nicely. Come on, I'll show you where to go."

I follow her, forcing my stride to laid-back speed. We walk along the dock where Sea-Doos are getting gas and several people are eating on the picnic tables set up near the water.

She opens a screen door that leads to the cafe. All the tables are full, so she waves me to the counter and pats a stool. I sit and she takes the one next to me, calling out, "Myrtle?"

A woman with gray hair and one of the whitest smiles I've ever seen sticks her head through a door that I assume leads to the kitchen. "Yes, dear?"

"We have a polite request for the breakfast menu. You okay with that?"

The woman glances at me, raising an eyebrow as if she's wondering why Analise has taken such a special interest in a customer. "Put that way, of course I am. I just have to stay out of Miss Kat's way. She's got her Italian lunch special under way. What is it you'd like, son?"

"Pancakes?" I ask hopefully.

"Coming right up," she says, ducking back into the kitchen.

"She's nice," I say, not quite meeting Analise's gaze.

"She's the best," Analise agrees.

"Do you work here?"

"I do. For the summer."

"Aren't you pretty far from home? I mean I noticed your accent—"

"Actually, this is home now. I moved here about a month ago to live with my dad."

"Oh. That must be a big change for you."

"I love it here. It's so different from England."

"I'm sure."

"Where are you from? Originally, I mean?"

"L.A."

"Ah. That's a different world for sure."

"One I miss," I admit.

"Girlfriend there?"

I consider my answer, but opt for the truth. "Yes. Not a very happy one, but yes."

"She must miss you."

"I guess."

"Do you miss her?"

"I—yeah," I say, even though I'm not altogether sure of the reasons.

"Do you Skype and stuff?"

I nod. "Not quite the same though."

"Long distance is hard. That's why I wanted to move here to be with my dad. Talking to him on the computer wasn't enough."

"What about your mom?"

"She's still in England. She has a busy life. My dad was sick. He had a brain tumor, and we thought he might not make it."

"Wow. I'm sorry. I hope he's okay."

"He is. He married the woman who owns this marina. He's actually opening up a practice here on the lake. He's really excited about it. And I have a brother who's back in England and a new sister named Kat. She's the one cooking in the back. I think she's going to be the next Rachael Ray."

"Do you two get along?"

"She's awesome. It's like I didn't just get a sister but a best friend."

"That's really cool."

"It is," she agrees. "Do you have brothers or sisters?"

"A sister," I say without elaborating.

"Is she here too?"

"No. She—to be honest, I'm not really sure where she is."

Analise looks startled by this, but there's something about her that makes me want to be completely up front. Maybe because she's so open.

Myrtle appears with a plate of pancakes stacked four high. "There you go, young man," she says. "I hope you enjoy them."

"They look amazing," I say, my stomach reminding me that I'm hungry.

She puts a bottle of syrup next to the plate. "Glass of milk to go with that?"

"That would be great," I say.

She's back in a few moments with a tall glass of cold milk. I thank her before she heads for the kitchen.

"Would you like to eat alone?" Analise asks.

"Not if you don't mind watching me devour these."

She laughs. "Myrtle's cooking has that effect on people."

I eat then while she tells me some things about the lake area, the ski club that she's become a part of. "You should join us," she says. "It's really fun."

"I've never water-skied."

"We'll teach you."

"But everyone in the group is probably like expert level."

"We have a couple of beginners. You look athletic. I bet you'd catch on quick."

"I don't know," I say, wanting to, but at the same time, not wanting to look like a goober in front of her.

"We're meeting at six this evening. There's a cove where we have a course set up, and by that time, the water is smooth as glass. I can pick you up."

I should probably say no. I feel sure Mandy wouldn't be happy about me accepting Analise's invitation, but it's just a friend thing, so what's the harm. "If you're sure I won't look like a fool," I say.

"We'll make sure of it," she says, smiling a really appealing smile. "Just tell me where to pick you up."

*

A photograph can be an instant of life captured for eternity that will never cease looking back at you.
– Brigitte Bardot

Keegan

EVAN HAS MADE himself scarce for most of the afternoon, staying upstairs with his laptop. I put away the groceries I'd gotten at the store and then unpack a few stray boxes left from the moving truck.

One is full of photo albums. I almost decide to leave it for later. These are Evan and Reece. I pull one out, open the cover and feel my heart dissolve a little at the sight of the two of them in the bathtub, suds piled high on their heads, enormous smiles lighting up their faces.

I've never been good at looking back. It makes me sad for what was. Even so, I find myself taking the album over to a chair by the window, sitting down, and flipping to the second page.

They were such beautiful little children. I know I'm prejudiced, but it's true. So full of innocence and joy for life. Was there a specific moment when that changed? It seemed as if it was overnight. That one day they were children, happy and open to whatever fun thing I had planned for them. And the next, resistant and closed off.

Was it something I had done?

I've asked myself this question a thousand times.

Aside from working so much, was there something else I could have done to prevent them from shutting me out?

I honestly do not know the answer. I've rationalized many times that it is nature's way of preparing them to pull away, to go out and make lives of their own.

I suppose this is true on some levels. But with Reece, at least, it has been so much more.

I lift my gaze to the wide water view outside the window and think of the last day I saw my daughter. Of the anger in her expression and the way it transformed her into someone I truly did not know.

I had gotten home late that night. Filming had gone on until nine or so, and by the time I walked into the house, it was after ten. Reece had been waiting for me in the living room. Evan was out, a fact I would later be thankful for. I knew as soon as I looked at her that she was high on something. Her eyes were glassy, and her mouth had a slackness to it that I had never seen before.

Up until then, Reece had never let me see her under the influence of anything. We'd had confrontations about a couple of things I'd found in her room: a liquor bottle, cigarettes, what looked like the end of a joint.

She'd had explanations for all of it. It belonged to someone else. She had just wanted to try the cigarettes.

And maybe because it was what I wanted to hear, I believed her.

But that night, she'd made no pretense of hiding the fact that she was either drunk or high. And so I'd asked her outright, my voice noticeably uneven.

"What did you take, Reece?"

"Something to pass the time," she'd said, looking at me through accusing eyes. "Evan's gone. And you're never here."

"I was working late. You could have visited the set."

She rolled her eyes. "That's your thing, Mom. Not mine."

I flinched at the disapproval in her voice, forcing myself not to take it personally. She was a teenager, acting out. I walked over to the sofa and sat down next to her. "Maybe we should talk about that," I said.

"What? The fact that I'm directionless?"

"You didn't used to be, Reece. What's happened?"

"Maybe I just realized one day that I will never be able to live up to your standards, so why try?"

"Reece. That's not fair," I said. "I've only tried to help you figure out what you want to do with your life."

"I'm doing it."

"Not going to college. Disappearing for days at a time. Showing up here like this?" I fought to keep the anger from my voice. And I was angry. It felt as if Reece was simply throwing away every advantage she had been given. Advantages I never had.

Reece jumped up from the couch, staggering and hitting the edge of the coffee table.

"Reece!" I said. "What did you take?"

"Do you really think I would tell you that?" she snapped in a sharp voice. "All you need to know is that it was enough for me to find the courage to tell you what I needed to tell you."

I had never heard her sound so cold, so without feeling. I suddenly felt the blood leave my face. "What is it?"

She stared at me for several long moments before answering. "I'm pregnant. And I want to have an abortion. The only reason I'm telling you is that I don't have the money."

I literally sank back onto the sofa as if my legs had given way beneath me. "Reece."

"I know. You're so disappointed, right?"

I looked up at my daughter, feeling as if I did not know her at all. The disdain in her voice felt like a slap in the face. "You can't do that," I said. "Why would you—"

"It's my body, and I can do what I want," she said tightly, as if she had rehearsed this speech over and over again.

"You'll regret it," I said, tears welling in my eyes. "You don't have to do this. We'll figure something out."

"How would you know? Like you ever messed up when you were my age?"

"Reece," I said, "sit down, please."

Arms folded across her chest, she glared at me, but sat down on the far end of the sofa. "I do know," I said, my voice shaking.

"What do you mean?" she asked, looking at me as if she didn't know me.

I stared down at my hands, my fingers laced tightly together. "I was your age when I became pregnant with you."

"But you were married to my father. That's kind of different."

I couldn't say anything for a bit, struggling to find the right words. I made myself say them, even though doing so made me a liar. "I know I told you that your father and I were married for a short time. But—we weren't, sweetie."

"What do you mean?" she asked, her defiant posture from a few moments before disappearing altogether.

"We were dating, and when I told him I was pregnant with you, he said he wasn't ready to be a father. He wanted me to—"

"—have an abortion?" she finished for me.

I couldn't say it. Not in front of her. "Reece—"

"Did he really even die in a car wreck? Was that a lie too?"

"No," I said, even as I knew she had no reason to believe me. "He did. We were just never married."

"Why would you lie about that?" she asked, shaking her head, disbelieving.

"I didn't want you to feel unwanted," I said. And it was true. For a brief time, I had considered doing what her father, Rick, had wanted me to do. He'd said it was the only thing that made sense. Neither of us had money. I was still living with a foster family and hadn't finished high school.

"Even though it was true?"

"It wasn't true, Reece. I was very young and had no means of supporting myself, but somehow I knew that wasn't a choice I could live with."

"And you never regretted it?"

"Not even for a minute," I said.

And for a moment, just a single moment, I had seen in Reece's eyes the little girl who had once loved me with complete openness. A child who thought I could do no wrong.

I reached for her, wanting to pull her into my arms and hug her until she could believe that everything would be okay. It felt as if she wanted me to do exactly that, but then she pulled away and jumped to her feet, grabbing a jacket from the back of the sofa.

"I'm not you, Mom. I don't want a baby."

She ran out the door then, and I followed, running outside and trying to stop her before she backed out of the drive and pulled away.

But she was gone in an instant, and I stood there watching after her, fear for my child a choking knot in my throat.

I haven't seen her since that night. She'd come to the house one day when I was at work and Evan was in school, packed some of her clothes and taken them with her. She's cut me out of her life completely, and I have no idea how to get her back.

I close the photo album now, pressing my hand to the cover, wishing I had never opened up this door to the past. Grief hits me in the chest, and, for a few seconds, I feel as if I can't breathe.

I put the album back in the box and close the lid. These can wait until later. They will have to wait.

IT'S AFTER FIVE when I head down the two-lane state road for a run. Evan had made plans with someone he'd met at the dock earlier and rather than wait around to watch him leave, I decided running might help clear my head.

There's little traffic on the road, but I still run facing cars, stepping into the grass a couple of times when a vehicle passes in both lanes.

I notice Bowie's truck parked at the top of his driveway just as I round the curve before his house. He's standing at the mailbox, flipping through envelopes when he looks up and spots me.

I lift a hand to wave, and he waves back. He waits until I

reach his driveway, and I stop, leaning over to pull in some deep breaths.

"Quite a pace you've got going," he says.

"Thanks," I say, still winded. "Trying to outrun my brain."

"Is it working?"

"A little."

Carson sticks his head out the truck window and barks at me. Greeting or reprimand, I'm not sure. "Hi, Carson," I say.

He wags his tail, which in turn wags his body.

"How far are you running?" Bowie asks.

"Five, roundtrip."

"Good run."

"I'm not the fastest, but I don't mind distance."

He looks off for a moment, as if trying to decide whether he should say what he's about to say, and then, quickly, "I was going to cook something on the grill tonight. Care to join us?"

The invitation surprises me. My first inclination is to refuse because maybe he's just being polite, but then I think about the empty house waiting for me and the box of photo albums. I really don't want to go back there right now just to be alone. And so I say, "Sure. That sounds great. Why don't I finish out my run and I'll swing by on the way back? If you don't mind me being sweaty?"

"Not a problem. Okay," he says, "we'll see you in a few."

I start to jog off, then turn to look back at him. "Hey, Bowie."

"Yeah?"

"Thanks for the invitation."

"Thanks for accepting."

And with an inexplicably warm feeling in my chest, I run on.

*

Cruelty, like every other vice, requires no motive outside
of itself; it only requires opportunity.
– George Eliot

Bowie

WAS INVITING HER over the right thing to do?

I'm cleaning off the grill and putting foil on the racks when the question decides not to leave me alone.

I could try to fool myself into thinking it was an act of courtesy and nothing more, but that would be a waste of energy, since I know myself better than that.

I also know that I'm not one to set myself up for false hope. Thinking Keegan Monroe and I could become anything other than friendly neighbors is naive at best and gullible at worst.

I had continued my Netflix binge of her show last night. She's really good at what she does. Amazingly, I was able to forget for lapses of time that I had met her in person, that she really wasn't that fairly naughty character she had played on *Aimless*.

Even so, it had been a bit of a reality jolt to see her running down the road toward me, her dress and demeanor so very different from that character. There had been something in her eyes that prodded me to make the invitation despite my very-grounded belief that we were destined to be friends and nothing more. A sadness that was at definite visual odds with her life as her fans no doubt perceived it.

I wonder now if it had to do with her daughter, and somehow I know it does. I can't imagine how that must feel. Being rejected by your child.

"Hey."

I turn at the sound of her voice calling out from the front porch. "Hey," I say. "Didn't hear you come in."

Carson runs to greet her. I call him back, but he's intent on following through, wagging his tail so hard it's a blur.

She gives him a tentative pat on the head, but I can see that it's not something she's comfortable with. "Carson," I call out again.

This time he returns to my side, staring up at me with a questioning look as if he doesn't understand what he's done wrong. I rub him under the chin in our no-words-needed signal for "you're okay."

Keegan looks uncomfortable, as if she knows she has offended both of us, but doesn't know how to fix it. I'm struck by my own surge of awkwardness and say, "There's a bathroom on the main floor just past the kitchen. Plenty of clean towels in there if you'd like to make use of it."

"I am pretty sweaty," she says. "I didn't think about that when I accepted your invitation."

"No problem. Just make yourself at home."

"Thank you," she says and disappears into the house.

Carson whines. "You're fine," I say. "You can't expect to win the entire world over, you know."

But I have to say, I'm a little surprised by her standoffishness, since she did fix him a special plate last night. It's like having your child rejected.

In the kitchen, I start slicing vegetables, potatoes, onion, zucchini, and squash. I pull out a large stainless-steel baking sheet and begin piling them on top. I'm drizzling them with olive oil and sea salt when Keegan walks back into the kitchen.

"Much better," she says. "Thanks for the use of your bathroom. I hope you don't mind. I ducked into the shower for a minute."

Her words bring an instant visual to my mind. Keegan Monroe in my shower. Clothes on or off? Off, you dufus. But then the visual is back, evidence of it in the reddening of my face.

"Ah, no problem," I say, turning away and making a pretense of looking for something to stir the vegetables with.

"Any way I can help?" she asks.

"How are you with brown rice?"

"Outstanding."

"All right, then. There's a bag in the pantry there. Pots are in the drawer by the stove. You can get that underway while I put the veggies on the grill."

"Sounds great," she says, and I head outside, welcoming the cooling evening air and its ability to lessen the heat licking through my body.

Carson follows me out, as if he knows he won't be welcome in the kitchen with Keegan. I rub his head again, saying, "You know you're top shelf with me, right, buddy?"

He wags his tail and flops down beside the grill.

A few minutes later, Keegan sticks her head out the door and says, "Rice is underway. Is this bottle of wine up for consumption?"

"Absolutely," I call back. "Glasses are in the cabinet above the sink. Corkscrew in the silverware drawer. Bring it on out."

"Be right there," she says, ducking back inside.

I'm stirring the vegetables on the stainless sheet when she comes out with the bottle and glasses.

"Want to open it?" she asks, handing me the corkscrew. "I'm terrible about getting cork in the wine."

"I'm not the best, but I'll give it a try."

I insert the corkscrew and pull it out with a pop. She holds out the glasses and I fill them halfway.

"See," she says. "Perfect. No cork."

We toast to it, taking a sip of the wine.

"That's really excellent," she says. "I love red."

"I picked it up on a trip to a vineyard in Burgundy. Once you've developed a taste for the French stuff, there's no going back."

"I've never been. I've heard it's beautiful though."

"Have you done a lot of traveling?"

"Some. Mostly the kind where you go hide for a week or so and try to regroup. I've never done much of the adventurous kind of traveling."

"I love it," I say. "Although I've become kind of a homebody with Carson here. I hate to leave him in a kennel. It represents the end of the world to him."

"It would be a lot easier if you could explain that you'll be back."

"It would," I say, taking a sip of my wine and wondering again at the juxtaposition of her seemingly empathetic view of dogs and her reluctance to get near them.

"I'm sorry if I'm not as friendly as he's used to people being," she says, as if she's read my mind. "It's something I'd really like to get past, but can't seem to do."

"What do you mean?" I ask.

"I'm kind of scared of them," she admits, even though she

sounds embarrassed by the fact. "Logically, I know there's no reason to be scared of Carson. He's obviously a love."

"Mind if I ask why?"

She swirls her wine around the glass, staring down at it as if she's not sure how to find the words, before finally saying, "It was something that happened a long time ago."

I wait for her to go on, almost telling her she doesn't have to because I can tell whatever it is, it is a painful memory. And maybe it's something that will be helpful for her to say. So I wait.

"I grew up in foster homes. Several of them, actually. I'm sure there are really good foster families out there, but I seemed to end up in the ones who endured a never-ending revolving door of children because of the check they brought with them at the end of every month. I always wanted a puppy, but I didn't end up staying long enough with any one family for that to happen."

Her voice has gotten even, as if finding the will to recite this memory is more than difficult. I want to tell her to stop, but find that I can't because something deep inside me wants to know, even as I feel sure it's not something I'm going to want to hear.

"One of the families I lived with . . . the father . . . he was very strict. He came home from work one night, drunk as usual, and the wife told him I hadn't done my chores after school. I was twelve at the time, and he said I was too big to spank, so he had another punishment in mind for me. He dragged me out to his truck and threw me inside, daring me to get out. I was too scared to even try, but terrified the entire time he was driving us to somewhere I'd never been before."

Again, I want to stop her, but she's no longer looking at

me, staring out at the lake beyond as if she has slipped back to another time in her life.

"It was this awful place out in the country. A small building where I could hear dogs barking and snarling as soon as we pulled up. He said he was going to take me inside and let me learn a lesson I would never forget. I was crying and struggling to get away, but he just picked me up and carried me to the doorway where I could see two dogs in the middle of a dirt floor being forced to fight each other.

"He dragged me right up to one of them. The dog that was losing tried to get behind me to get away from the other dog, so I ended up being in the middle of them. I really thought they would tear me apart. He said if I didn't do what I was supposed to do around the house, he would bring me back out there and make sure that it happened."

I don't even know if she's aware of it, but tears are streaming down her face. My heart feels like someone has tied it up in a knot, and it has lost all ability to pump blood through my body. I set down my wine glass, and even though I am virtually a stranger to her, I want to comfort her.

I reach for her. "Come here," I say, pulling her into my arms and wrapping her tight against me. "I am so sorry that you ever went through something like that. My God, who could do that?"

She's crying softly now. I feel her tears seep into my shirt, wet my skin. I rub a hand across the back of her hair. I don't know what I imagined as her childhood, but looking at the success she's made of herself, it would never have been this.

She slips her arms around my waist, and we stand there for a long time holding each other. I don't want to move. I just want to be whatever support she needs for as long as she needs it. I'm not sure how much time has passed when a boat eases by close into the cove, and Keegan pulls away, wiping her face.

"What is it about you that makes me open my soul and drown you in personal details?"

I shake my head a little, saying, "I don't mind."

"You should," she says, sniffing. "All I've done since we met is force you into help mode."

"I don't see it like that," I say, wanting to touch her face again, but forcing myself not to. Distance has crept back in, and I can see that she's embarrassed at how much she's revealed of herself.

"As for you being scared of dogs, who wouldn't be after something like that?"

She shrugs, wiping the back of her hand across her face. "The sad thing was the dogs didn't want to fight. I could see it in their eyes. It was horrible."

A slow-burning rage ignites in my chest, and I'm reminded of so much of the evil I have seen from people who perpetrate crimes on the innocent. I feel the same helplessness I had so often felt in my work and wish for the ability to turn the tables.

Carson gets up from his snoozing spot and walks over beside us, looking up at Keegan and whining softly. It's as if he senses her suffering and wants to console her. She reaches out and puts a tentative hand on his head. He sits perfectly still, his tail making a soft swish-swish sound on the rock terrace.

"He's really special, isn't he?" Keegan says softly.

"I think he is," I say. "Of all the living beings I've met, dogs have the most incredible ability to just be what you need them to be."

She rubs his head again, and he gently licks the top of her hand.

I smell something burning, remember the vegetables and step back to open the grill. “Looks like they’re done,” I say, “with the exception of the edges.”

“They smell great,” she says. “I’ll go check on the rice.”

I watch her walk to the house, step onto the porch, and disappear inside. I glance at Carson, and I swear he’s got this look in his eyes. A look that makes it clear he knows I’m in trouble.

You can close your eyes to reality but not to memories.
– Stanislaw Jerzy Lec

Keegan

I MIGHT AS well write RUN on my forehead. It wouldn't be any less effective a method of scaring off Bowie Dare.

I turn down the rice and then head for the bathroom, where I rinse my face with cool water until I look at least a little more in control. I stare at myself in the mirror and wonder why I just told him all that. I've never told anyone else before.

Not even my children.

Evan just thinks I'm weird where dogs are concerned, and I'm not even sure why I've never shared the memory with him, except that it seemed like too awful a picture for me to paint of my childhood.

They know that I grew up in the foster-care system, but I've never shared any of the details with them, so I'm not sure they could imagine that things like that had happened to me.

I've never wanted them to feel sorry for me, never wanted anyone to for that matter. So why tell Bowie Dare? I have no answer except for the fact that I have a feeling he's seen far more horrible things than I could put in front of him.

As for seeing pity in his eyes? There had been none. Anger, yes. And if I'm not wrong, something like admiration. Which I can't begin to explain.

I towel my face dry, wish for some makeup and then roll my eyes at my own vanity. With everything I've just shown him, I hardly think makeup is going to cover up the imperfections.

*

There is no respect for others without humility in one's self.

– Henri Frederic Amiel

Evan

I IN NO WAY intended to put myself behind a ski boat when I agreed to go with Analise to her club meeting.

And yet here I am, holding onto the ski-rope and getting ready to do another face plant. The driver of the Ski Nautique is a surprisingly nice guy named Mark who has managed to keep from running the boat into a dock, even though he can't seem to keep his eyes off Analise.

Not that it's hard to understand.

She's sitting on the back of the boat, giving me advice on what to do differently every time I fall. I'm mostly taking it in, except for the moments when I fail to keep my gaze on her face instead of the bikini she's wearing.

And that is way easier said than done.

"Lean back a little more, Evan," she calls out over the low roar of the boat's engine. "You've almost got it. Really!"

I'm not anywhere near sure that I believe her, but I'm convinced that she knows what she's talking about, so I wait for the rope to lose its slack and give the signal that I'm ready.

The boat lunges forward, and I tilt back a little more this time against the yank of the rope. I teeter for a moment, but then regain my balance, and I'm up, skiing in the center between the wakes, on two skis, admittedly, but skiing!

"You've got it!" Analise calls out. "Woo-hoo!"

Mark throws a fist in the air, keeping his gaze straight ahead. Despite the fact that he obviously has a thing for Analise, he clearly takes his driving seriously.

I follow the boat to the end of the cove, swinging out to the right as it makes a turn to circle back. I cross the wake holding my breath, but manage to navigate the rise and fall without crashing.

I make two whole rotations of the course before Mark heads back to the dock, indicating with a wave when I should let go of the rope and glide to a stop just short of the group of people clapping for my success.

It's a little embarrassing since I've already seen some of them ski, on one, like pros, but then I guess they all started out on two.

The boat is back in a minute. Just as I look over my shoulder, Analise jumps into the water, landing next to me with a big smile on her face.

"That was awesome," she says.

"You're being kind. And generous," I say, smiling despite my desire to look cool about it.

"I've seen people take days to get up on two skis. You're a good athlete."

"Thanks. For the instruction and everything."

"You're welcome."

The boat lines up twenty yards or so away, and another skier prepares to take off.

We watch, floating in our life jackets. The boat hits it, and the skier, a girl in a skimpy orange bikini hits the water with expert skill, dipping to the right and zooming out the side, cutting hard, and then zipping back across the wake.

"Wow," I say.

"She skis competitively," Analise says. "Great, huh?"

"Yeah. She must have started really young."

"She did. And she loves it."

"That's obvious."

"I'm not a native here myself. But it's been pretty easy to make friends. There's something to that saying that people are friendly in the south."

"And you think it's more exciting here than England?"

She tips her head, her blue eyes on mine. "In some ways, yes. I'm different here."

"How so?"

"I went to a private school there. I guess there was a lot of emphasis on who has what."

"Try L.A."

She laughs. "I can imagine. But you miss it?"

"Why do you say that?"

"You just remind me of me when I first decided to stay here with my dad."

"How's that?"

"You don't think it will ever compare."

"I don't see how it could."

"I didn't either. But I don't think we get it until we experience it, you know? People are just more easygoing here. I mean, don't get me wrong. There's plenty of teenage drama you can get involved in, if you want to. I just kind of decided I don't want to be involved in it."

"You sound older than you are."

She shrugs, as if she agrees this is true. "I've grown up a lot in the past year or so."

I can tell this isn't a casual statement. "You mean because of your dad?"

"Yeah," she says, floating on her back and staring up at the sky. She skims her hands across the water. She bumps my shoulder with her fingertips, and I feel a stab of electricity surge through me.

"Is he just like he was before—" I break off there, feeling as if I'm getting too personal. "Sorry."

"No," she says. "He had some memory loss. Some of them came back. Some didn't. But other than that, he's pretty great. And I'm going to have a new baby brother."

"Wow."

"I know. I'll be so much older than he is. But maybe that's good in some ways. I can take him places and teach him stuff."

"That's really cool." I think about Mandy, realizing how very different she is from Analise. And I can't help questioning the differences. Mandy is a lot more worldly than Analise. I thought I liked that about her. Do I?

"Why don't you have a boyfriend?" I ask, diverting my own thoughts.

"How do you know I don't?"

The question catches me up, and I stutter a regretful, "I mean, I assumed he would be around if you did."

"You're right about that. So no, I don't. At the moment."

"Why?"

"Because I'm picky."

"And honest," I say, laughing a little.

"Why shouldn't I be?"

"You should, actually. I'm sure you could take your pick. Mark sure seems to like you."

"He's sweet," she says. "But he's not my type."

"What's your type?"

"I figure I'll know him when I see him."

"I'm not sure I've ever met anyone like you," I say.

"Good," she says, smiling. "I like being an original."

She splashes water at me, hitting me in the face.

"Hey," I say.

She takes off swimming away from me, laughing as she goes. I swim after her, grabbing her ankle and pulling her back to me.

She tries to dunk me, and I let her, going under the surface with a gurgle. When I come back up, she's laughing. And we both go still for a moment, looking into each other's eyes. I feel the shift inside me, the realization that I haven't felt this kind of attraction before.

And I could be wrong, but I'm pretty sure I see it in her eyes as well.

*

Blame is just a shame game.
– Author Unknown

Keegan

"THE FOOD IS wonderful," I say, accepting a second portion of grilled veggies on my plate.

"Good," Bowie says. "Nice job on the rice too."

"It's hard to mess up rice," I say.

"Not true. You can burn it. Undercook it. Overcook it, but not burn it."

I laugh. "Okay. So I'm great with rice. How'd you get so good with the grill?"

"Practice. I like being outside. So cooking outside is always my first choice."

"Except in the winter?"

"Even then if it's not too cold."

"You're here year round?"

"Unless I have a trip planned, yep."

"I hear the winters can get rough."

"They seem to either end up being mild or pretty harsh. I haven't seen a lot of in between. Did you grow up in California?"

"No. Actually, I grew up in D.C."

"So you do know cold winters."

I nod. "One thing I will miss about L.A. is the climate."

"What else?"

"Will I miss?"

He nods.

"Not the traffic, that's for sure."

"What about your work? With the kind of success you've had, won't you miss that?"

"Maybe eventually. Right now, I just kind of feel the need to regroup. I'm really not sure what I'm going to feel in a year or two."

"Can I ask you a personal question?"

"Sure, although I can't imagine that you want to hear any more personal details about me tonight."

"Are you punishing yourself?"

The question takes me by surprise. It implies an insight that it's not easy to dodge. Even so, I try. "What do you mean?"

"I just wonder if you left that show because you think you somehow caused your daughter's rebellion."

"I—" I get no further than that because I don't think I could convince him any more than I've convinced myself. "I wish I'd eased up on the ambition at some point. Had more time with her and with Evan."

He looks at me for several long moments. I can feel him assessing my answer the way he might have assessed a suspect in a case. "Do they know about your childhood?"

Again, the question surprises me, and I have to wonder why he would assume I hadn't told them. "Not too much of it," I admit. "Why do you ask?"

"Because it seems like your daughter would understand your work ethic a little better if she knew how different your life was from hers."

"On this side of it, I can see that. I don't know, when they were growing up, I just never wanted them to have to think about me in that way. I wanted them to feel the kind of security I never felt." I hesitate, and then add, "I didn't want to bring the ugliness of my childhood into their lives."

"What happened to your parents?" he asks, his voice soft, caring.

"They were drug addicts. They both died of overdoses, at different times, but same ending."

"I'm sorry, Keegan. That sucks."

"It does," I say. "I was young. Four when she died. Six when my dad died. I don't have too many memories of them. And honestly, the ones I do have I'd just as soon not."

We're quiet for a bit, and I have the feeling that he's digesting what I've said, trying to find the right thing to say.

"Please don't feel sorry for me," I finally get out. "I hate the thought of being pitied."

"I don't feel sorry for you," he says then. "I'm actually admiring you. I can't imagine how hard you must have worked to get where you've gotten in life. It's not easy to make it in this world even with extreme advantages. Give yourself credit for that. You're obviously a really strong person."

I shake my head and laugh a little. "Sometimes, we don't have a choice, do we?"

"But not everyone holds up to the test. You did. You have."

"Well, now I know where to come when I'm down on myself," I say, trying to put a teasing note in my voice, but not exactly succeeding.

"Yeah, you do," he says. "You're really good at what you do. That doesn't happen without a lot of hard work."

"And how would you know?" I ask, tipping my head and smiling.

He smiles back. "Netflix. I'm now an *Aimless* groupie."

I laugh and spear another zucchini with my fork. "Who's your favorite character?"

"Aside from yours?"

I nod.

"Amos."

"He's crazy, isn't he?"

"But good crazy," Bowie says. "In a Robin Hood kind of way. I can see why you're—I mean your character—is in love with him."

I laugh again, and we talk for a good long while about the show, on set and off. He's interested in things I don't often share with others. And it's then that I realize I haven't had someone to talk to like this in a really long time. It's nice. And comfortable. And as the darkness overtakes the evening, I think the best thing I've done in a good while was stopping to ask Bowie Dare for directions.

*

After great pain, a formal feeling comes. The Nerves sit
ceremonious, like Tombs.
– Emily Dickinson

Bowie

I KNOW I'M getting in over my head.

I'm a rational guy. It's just how my brain works. It made me good at my job and might be the reason why I'm able to write characters who people seem to identify with. I kind of know when something is going to work and when it's not.

For now, right here in this moment, or even in this upcoming summer of moments, Keegan and I might work.

There's attraction here. Both physical and otherwise. I'm drawn to her in ways I've haven't been drawn to anyone since my marriage ended. And I think she's attracted to me as well. I've seen flashes of it in her eyes several times tonight.

But rational tells me that she's here to get to some place she needs to be. That staying here past that time is not likely.

We're drying dishes in the kitchen, quiet as we do. And I'm glad she can't hear what I'm thinking.

Once everything is put away, I expect her to say she needs to go, and I'll drive her home. But instead, she says, "I'd love to see a little of the lake by boat. Would you mind taking me out for a short ride?"

"Ah, sure," I say. "The full moon is always nice to see it by."

We walk to the dock, a couple of feet between us, Carson in front of us, tail wagging at this unexpected night outing.

"He loves the boat," I say. "It's his favorite thing to do."

"He's a great friend to you, isn't he?" Keegan says, and there's sincerity in her voice, maybe a little envy as well.

"We kind of get each other." I push the lift button, and the boat starts to lower in its hanger.

"How so?" she asks.

"His main goal in life is to enjoy every minute of every day. I kind of swore to myself when I left the FBI that was what I would do. Enjoy every minute of every day."

The boat touches the water, and I cut the power to the lift. Carson jumps in, and I hold out a hand to help Keegan step in. I back the boat out of the slip and ease across the glass-smooth water, heading out of the cove to the wider part of the lake. The moon is huge, throwing light across the surface and accentuating the beauty of this place I love.

"Can I ask you a personal question?" Keegan asks, as if she's been considering the life goal I share with my dog.

"Of course," I say.

"Did something happen to make you leave?"

I steer the boat a little closer to the shore, gliding past house after house, some lit up, others not. I consider giving her the standard answer I give when I'm asked why I left, but she's been honest with me tonight about things I know were hard to admit.

Maybe it's this that leads me to say, "There was this little girl who was taken from her home in the middle of the night in northern Virginia. She was asleep in her bed when a man came in through a window and abducted her. She was six. I was involved in the case from the beginning. Those first twenty-four hours, we were sure we would find her because we had reason to believe the abductor was a man who had worked for a contractor hired to refinish floors in the house the week before."

I stop for a moment, stare out across the lake, as the memory engulfs me, bringing with it all the old feelings of horror.

"You don't have to finish," Keegan says softly, and I can tell she's sorry she asked.

But I go on anyway because now that I've started, I want her to know about that beautiful little girl. "We followed false lead after false lead," I say. "And then one day, the parents received a note telling them their daughter was alive and where to find her. When we reached the location, we found her tied to a chair. She was alive, but her eyes had been removed. She was holding a note that said it had been necessary so that she wouldn't be able to identify him. Otherwise, he would have had to kill her and he didn't want to do that."

A sob slips from Keegan's throat. I glance at her, see the tears streaming down her face and slip the boat into park, cutting the engine.

I reach out and cover her hand with mine. "I'm sorry. I shouldn't have told you that."

She looks down at our joined hands. "How can such evil exist?"

"I don't know the answer to that. I just know that it does."

"Did they find the man?"

"No. He still hasn't been found. I haven't stopped working on it though."

"What do you mean?"

"I keep looking for leads. Asking questions. One day, he'll mess up. Get caught. I kind of live for that day."

Keegan turns her hand over, laces her fingers with mine.

"You shouldn't blame yourself, you know. For walking away. That's not the kind of thing a person can deal with but so many times."

"I think certain people have the ability to compartmentalize things. Separate them so that they can be effective in their jobs, but not take it home at night. I wasn't one of those people. I ended up in a psychiatric hospital for a month after that case."

"Bowie. I'm sorry."

I shrug. "It showed me that I have a line. I guess I pushed myself across it too many times, and all the good chemicals in my body leaked away. The world just looked gray and hopeless."

She shakes her head. "Most people have no idea of the horrific things that go on around them."

"And they don't want to."

A fishing boat glides by in the distance, the only sound registering in the night darkness.

"I can hear in your voice," Keegan says, "that you somehow think you failed in your career there."

I shrug. "Lots of people stick it out. My ex-wife thought I should be able to."

"When did you divorce?"

"After my stay in the hospital. The experience was a little much for her."

"I'm sorry, Bowie."

"It's for the best. I was somehow diminished in her eyes after that. She wanted a hero, and I was no longer that."

"That's not true," she says. "We're all meant to make a difference in the ways that are most true to ourselves. Feeling empathy for suffering makes you more human, not less."

"Someone has to fight the bad guys though."

"And you did. For how many years?"

"Fourteen."

"That's a long time."

"I won't deny that. I don't regret my decision to leave. It actually wasn't a choice."

"Sometimes, the next path we're meant to take isn't a choice. It's where we're supposed to be."

She stands then, unlinking our hands. She leans on the windshield of the boat, staring across the moon-lit water. "I think my coming here is one of those things."

I stand up beside her, looking out in the same direction. "It's kind of like once we get to the place we need to be, we get it. It's not so easy to see until we get there though."

She shifts slightly so that she is half facing me. "Bowie?"

I turn just enough that we are facing each other. "Yeah?"

"Would you kiss me?"

To say that the question surprises me doesn't get anywhere near accurate. I look down into her beautiful face and know that I have never wanted to kiss a woman so much in my life. I reach out and rub my thumb across her full lower lip.

A small sigh escapes her.

"Keegan—"

"Don't talk," she says. "Just kiss me."

So I do. With a tentative question at first. And then I just close my eyes. And we both get lost in it.

She slides her arms around my neck, locks herself tight against me.

It's a first kiss, and yet somehow familiar, in the way of something you've been waiting for, but until this point couldn't identify.

All I know is that I am suddenly filled with this awareness that something between us has clicked into place, compassion, understanding, a desire to acknowledge that, to be filled up by it.

I hook my hand to the back of her neck and deepen the kiss until we are both breathing hard and wanting more.

A thumping noise sounds from the back of the boat. We pull away from each other to see Carson looking at us and wagging his tail against the seat.

Keegan smiles and says, "That sounds like approval."

"His version of clapping," I say.

We both laugh, and Carson thumps his tail harder.

"As much as I would like to stay here and pick up where we left off," she says, "I should get home. I'm not sure when Evan is coming back."

"Yeah," I say. "Probably a good idea."

I drop into the driver's seat and turn on the boat.

She leans down and brushes her lips across mine. "I wasn't just saying that. I really would like to stay."

I look into her eyes and see that she means it. And I let her see that I'm glad.

*

I almost wish we were butterflies and liv'd but three summer days—three such days with you I could fill with more delight than fifty common years could ever contain.
–John Keats

Keegan

THE NEXT FEW days are the perfect definition of summer. Mornings are warm. Afternoons are hot. I read a book a day out on the dock, stretched out in the warm sunshine. Evan sometimes joins me, but is more often gone than not.

He's made some friends with the local ski club and is actually excited about his growing ability to keep up with them. I'm just happy to see him involved in something that has distracted him from thinking about how much he hates being here.

And, of course, I'm thinking about Bowie. I sent him a text the morning after our night on the lake, thanking him for the dinner and the conversation. He'd texted back with a polite "you're welcome, very much enjoyed it." But I haven't heard from him since, and I've convinced myself that the next move needs to be his.

I initiated the kiss—I did that—was it too soon? I don't know, but for now, I'm going to err on the side of taking it slow.

My agent sends texts announcing two new projects he thinks I'm perfect for. I copy and paste my previous answer, wondering when he will accept that I'm not interested. Not now. I don't know if ever.

I'm starting novel four on Saturday afternoon when my cell phone rings. It's lying on the floor of the dock beneath my chair. I reach for it, recognizing Bowie's cell number.

I swipe the screen, say hello with a nervous jitter in my stomach that ripples through my voice.

"Hey," he says. "This a good time?"

"Yes," I say. "Hey, Bowie. How are you?"

"Good. Just wondered if you'd like to go to lunch at Hayden's, the marina I mentioned."

"Evan's out again, and I'm actually beginning to tire of my own company. That sounds great."

"Good," he says. Is that relief in his voice?

"Pick you up in twenty minutes?"

"By boat?"

"Yeah."

"Okay. I'll be at the dock."

"See you in a few," he says.

I close my book, realizing there's a smile on my face.

I SEE HIM as soon as he rounds the bend that leads into our cove. He's got the boat wound out. Carson is up front, his ears flying back in the wind.

Bowie glides to a stop just short of the dock, raising his hand in a wave. "Hey," he says.

Carson barks.

I wave at them both, trying to keep my eyes on Bowie's face so that I don't look at his mouth and think about what it was like to kiss him.

He's wearing swim shorts and a T-shirt, his hair standing up a little from the wind. His shoulders are noticeably wide, and his arms are defined with muscle. I glance away as he takes my hand while I step onto the boat.

Carson trots over to greet me. I reach down and rub his ear. He rewards me with a lick on the back of my hand. I look up at Bowie then and see that he's just about to call Carson back, but I say, "It's okay. It's nice to be welcomed like that."

I sit down on the seat next to the driver's chair, looking out behind us as Bowie pulls away from the dock and hits the throttle until we're zipping across the water.

Lots of boats are out for the summer weekend. Sailboats drifting lazily along with the help of a light breeze. Sea-Doos cut back and forth, looking for the roughest water to allow for the most airborne antics. A skier rides behind a sleek-looking boat roaring up behind us.

Bowie glances in the rearview mirror, stares for a moment and says, "Isn't that Evan?"

I look closely then, saying, "It is! Wow, he's doing great!"

We both wave then as the boat cuts by on the left, a young girl driving. Evan spots us, lifts a hand to wave and promptly tips forward into a face plant.

"Oh, no!" I say, feeling terrible for him.

"We'll zip back and make sure he's okay."

We glide to a stop just short of the ski boat. The pretty girl driving lifts a hand, no doubt wondering who we are.

"That's my mom," Evan calls out from behind the boat. "And Mr. Dare. And Carson."

The girl looks at us and smiles openly. "Hello. Nice to meet you. I recognize you from the marina, Mr. Dare. I'm Analise. Sam Tatum is my dad."

"Nice to meet you," we both say in unison.

"I'm a regular at the cafe," Bowie says. "The cooking over there is ruining me. In fact, we're headed over for lunch now."

"It smelled good when I left," she says.

"Skier down back here," Evan yells, teasing.

"Sorry about that," I direct back at him. "You looked good though."

"I have a long way to go, but Analise is a good teacher."

"All right then, we'll leave you to it." I feel Analise's gaze linger on my face.

"Oh, my gosh," she says. "You play on *Aimless*!"

"Did," I say.

"Evan!" Analise admonishes. "How could you not tell me that?"

"It's not really his kind of show," I say, trying to cover up the awkward moment.

"But you're his mom, and that's fabulous!"

"Thanks. We didn't mean to interrupt the skiing," I say. "And we're headed for lunch."

"Okay," Analise says. "Well, I'm a big fan!"

"Thanks," I say again, deciding that she seems really sweet. "Have fun out here," I add to them both. And we head out.

*

You cannot find peace by avoiding life.
– Virginia Woolf

Bowie

"DID THAT BOTHER you?" I ask once we've pulled away and taken off across the water.

"What?" she asks.

"That Evan hadn't mentioned the show."

"Actually, it doesn't. It makes me think he just sees me as his mom. And that's all I've ever wanted either of my children to see me as."

I don't know why the answer is surprising, but it is a little. "They're lucky to have you as a mom."

She shrugs, looks off to the side of the boat. When she turns back to face me, she says, "I wish I could say they would agree with you."

The no-wake buoys for the marina are just ahead. I slow the boat so that we float in without a wake. "You shouldn't be so hard on yourself, Keegan. I don't think the teenage phase is easy for anyone, but having met Evan, you've done a lot of things right."

"Thanks," she says. "I guess sometimes it really is hard to see the forest for the trees."

Ahead, a young girl is helping tie up boats in front of the marina. I point her out to Keegan, saying, "That's Kat, Analise's stepsister now. Gabby and Sam Tatum own the marina here. They've been married a short while and are expecting a baby."

"I met her at the farmer's market up the road," Keegan says. "Gabby, I mean. She was really nice."

"Theirs is one of those stories that make you believe in meant to be. They dated in high school, and I'm not sure of all the details, but found each other again not that long ago."

We're almost to the dock when Keegan looks at me and says, "Do you believe in that?"

"What?"

"Meant to be."

I look into her eyes and feel myself falling as if someone has physically pushed me from a cliff. My response is surprising to my own ears. "Yeah," I say. "I think I do."

*

Be kind whenever possible. It is always possible.
– Tenzin Gyatso, 14th Dalai Lama

Keegan

THE YOUNG GIRL who helps us tie up the boat is all the advertisement this marina will ever need to keep people coming back. She greets us with a wide, beautiful smile, her long blonde hair hanging in a braid over her left shoulder.

"Hey, Kat," Bowie says. "This is my friend Keegan. Keegan, this is Kat."

"Hi," the girl says, sticking out her hand. We shake, and she says, "You play on that show."

I smile at her and nod. "Nice to meet you, Kat."

"Wow. You too. Wait 'til I tell Mom we have a celebrity at the marina."

"I met your mom the other day. We had a nice chat."

"Cool," Kat says. And then to Bowie, "Hope you're in the mood for something Italian today."

"What's the special?" he asks.

"Panzanella."

"That bread salad you make?"

"Yep," she says, looking proud.

"And what's Myrtle going to surprise us with?"

"She has fried green-tomato sandwiches today," she says with a smile.

"Who's selling the most?" Bowie asks.

"Right now, Myrtle," she concedes.

Bowie laughs. "I'll be taking you up on the panzanella."

She gives him a high-five, asking, "Do you need gas in the boat?"

"You could fill it up," he says.

"Will do."

We walk inside the marina cafe, and the smells are instantly intoxicating. "Oh, my goodness," I say. "I am suddenly starving."

"Then we're at the right place."

"Hey, Mr. Dare!" a woman calls out from behind a serving counter. "Y'all have a seat anywhere."

"Thanks, Myrtle," he says, and we take a table by the window that looks out over the lake.

A pretty young waitress hands us two menus. Bowie tells her he'll have the panzanella special. I opt for the fried green-tomato sandwich. We both ask for unsweetened iced tea.

"I can't believe I just ordered that," I say, shaking my head.

"When in Rome," he says.

I glance around the cafe, feeling the charm of the place, the low voices of other customers a hum in the background. "I love this," I say.

"It's my favorite place to eat around here," Bowie says. "The Tatums have expanded the kitchen and the seating area. It just keeps getting more popular."

"I can see why," I say.

The door opens, and a couple walks inside. I instantly recognize Gabby Tatum. She spots me at the same time, waves and takes the man with her by the hand to lead him over to us.

"Hi," she says, smiling in a way that makes me realize she's glad to see me. "I was hoping you would come by. Hey, Bowie," she says.

"Hey, Gabby. Sam," Bowie says.

"Oh, sorry, honey," she says, tucking her arm into his. "Sam, this is Keegan. I told you that we met at the farmer's market."

He sticks out his hand and warmly shakes mine. "Nice to meet you," he says.

"You, too," I say, noticing that he is as handsome as Gabby is beautiful. "What a great place this is."

"You're new to the lake?" he asks.

"Yes. My son and I bought a house not too far from here. Actually, we just met your daughter. She's pulling my son, Evan, skiing out on the lake."

Sam's eyebrows raise a bit. He looks at Gabby and shakes his head, smiling. "That must be her new friend. Evan. The one she can't stop talking about."

"Ah," I say. "They appear equally smitten."

"Would you like to join us?" Bowie asks, waving a hand at the empty chairs at our table.

"We would love to," Gabby says. "But we're on the way to Roanoke for an appointment. Just checking in with Myrtle before we go. I really hope you enjoy the lunch. We'd love to have you over for dinner if there's a time that works for you."

"Thanks," I say. "That sounds wonderful."

"Then we'll do it," Gabby says, waving as they leave.

"Is everyone here that nice?" I ask Bowie once they're out the door.

"There are a lot of nice people here," he says. "You'll find an exception here and there, but it's one thing I like about living in this area. It's not like a big city where it's hard to run into someone you know."

The waitress arrives with our plates. Bowie's panzanella salad fills a large white bowl and my fried green-tomato sandwich is enormous. "Oh, my," I say.

Bowie smiles. "You might have some to take home with you."

We don't waste any time getting started on our food. And it's so good that conversation isn't on either of our minds. But I can only finish half of my sandwich.

"That was unbelievable," I say, putting a hand on my very full belly.

The woman from the kitchen comes out, a wide smile on her face. "What's the verdict today, Mr. Dare? And who is this pretty lady you have with you?"

"Extraordinary from both of us, I think," Bowie says, looking up at her with with a grin. "And this is Keegan Monroe. Keegan, Myrtle is one of the fine chefs here."

"Nice to meet you," I say. "This was amazing."

She glances at what's left of my tomato sandwich. "Now you're gonna take that with you, aren't you?"

"Yes, ma'am," I say.

"And what did you think of that sauce? Too much jalapeno?"

"Not a bit. I loved it."

"I like her," Myrtle says, putting a warm hand on my shoulder and smiling at Bowie. "You bring her back anytime."

"Will do, Myrtle," Bowie says.

The cafe door opens, and an older couple walk in. "Hey there, Mr. and Mrs. Miller!" Myrtle calls out. "Find you a table, and we'll be right with you."

She's back to the kitchen then, humming as she goes.

"I think that's how a person should feel about their work," I say.

"What's that?" Bowie asks, pushing his bowl away, even though he hasn't quite finished it either.

"Like humming. Because they're happy doing it."

"Did you love your work?" he asks.

"I did for a lot of years. But the last few, I didn't hum very much anymore."

"Is that how you knew you wanted to leave the show?"

"You want an honest answer even though it's one you're not likely to believe?"

"Yeah," he says.

"I love acting. It's just something I enjoy doing. Like dancing, I guess. Or creating music. But I started to feel like maybe I wasn't doing it for the right reasons anymore. It no longer needed to be about the money. I started to wonder if my ego liked the glory stuff a little too much."

He looks at me for a few moments, shaking his head. "That's honest. But I have to say you don't seem to take yourself that seriously."

I shrug. "I don't want to. But there's something about people you don't know, people who know next to nothing about you other than the role you play, acting as if you're worthy of adoration that makes you start to think maybe you are. That maybe the world really needs to know what designer you're wearing, who your stylist is and what you eat for breakfast."

Bowie laughs a little. "And you don't think the world really needs to know those things?"

"No. None of that will promote a morsel of good on this planet."

"Is that what you want now? To promote good?"

"If I can. I'm not sure how yet."

"I bet you'll know it when it comes along."

"I hope so."

He's quiet again, and then says, "Do you think you need to justify what you've earned for yourself, Keegan?"

I consider the question. "Maybe."

"Maybe being kinder to yourself might be a good place to start."

I could take the assessment as criticism, but it's not intended that way. I can tell from the look in his eyes. And so I take it as it's meant. An observation rooted in compassion.

*

Four things come not back: The spoken word, The sped arrow, The past life, The neglected opportunity.
– Arabian Proverb

Evan

IT'S LATE AFTERNOON when Analise pulls the boat into a cove near the foot of Smith Mountain. There are no houses built along the waterfront. She drops the anchor just out from a stretch of sandy white beach.

"How about a swim?" she asks.

"Sure," I say, averting my eyes as she pulls off her T-shirt and shorts.

Before I can pull off my own shirt, she's jumping over the side of the boat, splashing water back on me.

"Hey," I say and jump in after her.

We chase each other around, dunking and splashing, until, laughing, we swim in to the beach and sit on the sand, facing the lake. I'm out of breath, wiping water from my face when I say, "You're tough."

"Have to be with a big brother."

"What's he like?" I ask.

"He's the good one," she says.

"And you're the bad one?"

"Not so much anymore," she says, tipping her head. "But, yeah, I was."

"You don't seem like the bad one," I say.

"I gave my mom and dad a hard time for a few years."

"How so?"

"Getting into anything I thought would annoy them."

"Why?"

"Because they got divorced, and I got lost, I guess. Cliche, I know, but maybe that was the only way I could think to get attention."

"What changed?"

"My dad getting sick," she says, her voice serious. "You think you can imagine what it would be like to lose someone you love. To not have them in your life anymore. But you really can't. Not until it's real, and you have to face it."

"Yeah," I say. "That's tough."

"It wasn't as tough for me as it was for my dad. He's the one who had to face the reality of dying. But it changed me too. It changed all of us, actually."

I think about my mom then, wonder if I've been taking her for granted. I know my sister has, but have I acted much better? Not a lot.

"I probably have some work to do in that department," I say.

"With your mom, you mean?"

I nod.

"It did seem a little weird that you didn't mention she was an actress."

"Why do you say that?"

Analise shrugs. "It seems like you'd be really proud of her. I would be."

"I am," I say, but I can't deny that I should give my mom more credit than I do.

"Can I give you some advice?" Analise asks.

"Sure."

"Don't wait," she says. "Because you never know. You just never know."

"You sound a lot older than you are," I say, tracing a finger through the sand between us.

"I guess I've grown up a good bit in the past year. When I think about how I treated my dad before he got sick." She shakes her head and says in a low voice, "I was such a brat."

"Maybe you didn't mean to be?"

"Oh, I meant to be," she says, smiling a little.

"We are teenagers," I say. "Maybe we're a little bit entitled?"

She shrugs. "All I know is there was a point when I thought I might not have a chance to have a good relationship with my dad again. That would have been a horrible thing to have to live with."

"I'm glad you didn't have to."

"Me, too." We meet eyes for a moment, before we both glance off like we're shy or something. I haven't felt shyness with a girl since I was like eleven.

"Are you an only child?" she asks.

"No. I have a sister," I say.

"Older?"

"Two years older."

"Where is she?"

"We don't really know."

Analise tips her head and says, "What do you mean?"

"She kind of decided she wanted to go her own way."

"You don't see her?"

"Not in almost a year."

"That must kill your mom."

"Pretty much."

"Did they have a fight or something?"

I look out at the lake where another boat is pulling a skier. "Reece got pregnant and told Mom she was having an abortion."

"Oh," Analise says. "Wow. That's some painful stuff."

"It is."

"Did she go ahead with it?"

"As far as I know. But like I said, we haven't seen her."

"You sound like you're mad at her."

I shrug. "It's just hard to think about, you know. That would've been my niece or nephew. And the baby didn't do anything wrong."

"So you think she should have kept the baby?"

"Or let Mom raise him or her."

"Would she have done that?"

"I'm pretty sure she would have. She was more than devastated about the whole thing."

We're quiet for a while. I notice the sound of the water lapping against our ankles, the roar of a SeaDoo engine somewhere out of sight.

"What would you do?" I find myself asking. "If it happened to you, I mean."

"Well, I believe we don't know for sure what we would do in a situation until we're really in it. But I know myself, and I . . . couldn't . . . I would give the baby up for adoption after it was born, if I couldn't keep it myself. There are so many people who can't get pregnant, and I guess it seems like that would be changing something that wasn't supposed to be into something that absolutely was meant to be."

I study her face for a good while, long enough that she sits back a bit, and with a soft smile, says, "What? Do I have mud on my nose or something?"

"No," I say. "I was just wondering if I could kiss you."

"Funny," she says. "I was just hoping you would."

And so I do. Just kissing. Neither of us touching each other beyond that. But then she makes a small sound of pleasure, and I reach out to put my arms around her waist and pull her to me. She shifts onto my lap and slips her arms around my neck.

The sun is hot on my shoulders, and I can feel it starting to burn my skin, just as I'm pretty sure I can feel this girl starting to burn my soul.

*

It's good to get silly, a bit willy-nilly. A person is only as old as his soul.
– Author Unknown

Bowie

I REALLY DON'T want to take her home just yet. I'm pretty sure I should because every time I'm with her, I'd like to be with her a little longer.

"There's a putt-putt course up at the other end of the lake. You up for a game?"

She looks at me and smiles, and I have to wonder if I really just invited her to play putt-putt.

"That sounds fun," she says. "I've never played."

"Never?"

She shakes her head.

"How about regular golf?"

"Nope."

"Should we play for money?" I ask, grinning a little.

"You're evil," she says.

"A man has to take his advantages where he can find them."

"Oh, is that right?"

"Yep."

"Well, I'm a fast learner, so I'll take that bet."

"All right, then," I say.

We both stand with the wind blowing against our faces as I point the boat toward the Hales Ford side of the lake. It's a good twenty-minute ride, even with the boat wound out. We don't talk. Keegan studies the houses and docks we're passing.

When we're close to Bridgewater Marina, I slow the boat for the upcoming no-wake zone.

"I had no idea the lake was this big," she says. "I mean I read about it, but it didn't sound as big as it actually is."

"There's been a lot of development in the last twenty years or so. My grandparents owned a good bit of land here before the dam was built. They lost a lot of it to the building of the lake, but still had a good bit of acreage."

"When was the dam built?"

"In the early sixties. For decades after that, it was mostly a fishing lake where people would bring boats in for the weekend. You'd see things like old school buses parked at the edge of the shore, and people would use them for a tent of sorts, I guess."

"The houses here now are so nice. How did people find out about the lake?"

"A local developer started doing some building. I guess he took a pretty big risk because there were a lot of doubters who said this lake would never support that kind of property. He built Bernard's Landing and Vista Point, the big high rise at the end of 626."

"Were they successful?"

I nod. "Things started to grow from there."

"It's not hard to see why people are drawn to moving here."

"Most people who do have no desire to leave."

"I could be one of those people," she says.

I focus my attention on pulling into a dock slip, not responding to that because I'm afraid if I do, it will be clear how much I hope it is true.

*

I have learned that to be with those I like is enough.
— Walt Whitman

Keegan

"SO YOU DIDN'T tell me you were a putt-putt shark," I say, watching him make another hole-in-one.

"We did put money on this, didn't we?" he teases.

"How does anyone even get this good at putt-putt?"

"Do I detect sore-loser syndrome?"

I laugh. "Maybe a little."

"I totally suck at regular golf. This is my version of trying to make myself feel better about that."

"It should be working for you," I say, aiming a ball at the hole and watching as it skitters off far to the left. "Oh, for goodness sake!"

Bowie laughs. "Should I spot you a few points?"

"Absolutely not," I say.

"Be happy to," he says.

I fume then while he finishes another section without missing a hole.

We play three rounds. Carson sleeps near the entrance to the course, Bowie walking over to check on him several times. It's dark when we finish the last round, and although I lose all three, I'm at least respectable by the end. I hand him the ten dollars, and he smiles, shaking his head.

"That's okay," he says. "I did take advantage of the fact that you'd never played."

"No, no. I pay my debts. You won fair and square," I say, forcing him to take the bill.

"How about I use it to buy us a pizza for dinner?" he asks, pointing at the restaurant just down the boardwalk.

So we head for the restaurant, Carson happily trotting along next to Bowie.

I find the restroom and stand in front of the mirror, looking at my disheveled hair and my red cheeks. I'm a mess, but staring at myself, I'm somehow okay with the way I look. I look relaxed, happy.

Those aren't things I've seen in myself in a very long time. It's actually kind of nice to think I still have them inside me. That I've found someone who likes who I am. Who seems to just like being with me.

And that's nice. Really nice.

*

Praise the bridge that carried you over.
– George Colman

Bowie

WE SIT AT an outdoor table, Carson flopping down next to my chair. The waitress recognizes Keegan, and she asks five minutes of questions before taking our order.

Keegan answers with politeness and an air of appreciation for the woman's interest.

Once we've given her our order and she's headed for the kitchen, I say, "You handle that really well."

"What?" she asks.

"People feeling like they know you because they've seen you on TV."

She shrugs a little and says, "I guess I understand it. I've felt that way about characters I've loved on shows I've watched. As actors, we want people to get so involved with the characters and their lives that they can't wait until next week's episode. So should we be surprised when they recognize us in real life and feel like they know some part of us?"

"I guess not," I say. "Seems like it would be hard to separate your personal life from it though."

"Most people are respectful of there being a line of sorts. I've just never understood celebrities who put themselves out in the public eye in the biggest ways possible and then act offended when people want their autographs or want to speak to them."

"I don't think you're typical of most celebrities, Keegan."

"Maybe it's about where you start in life," she says. "For most of mine, I could never imagine anyone being impressed enough with me to want my autograph."

"You're very gracious."

"I think grateful may be more accurate."

I study her for a few moments and say, "I don't think I've ever met anyone quite like you."

"I'm not that special, Bowie. I just enjoyed acting and was fortunate enough to find work that paid me for it."

"And you don't think it's unusual that you didn't start buying your own press somewhere along the way?"

"Most of us have days where we wake up thinking we're a little greater than we actually are. I've found it's better not to go there, because somehow life has a way of taking you down a notch or two."

"Can I be honest with you about something?"

"Sure."

"I didn't want to take you home this afternoon. I wanted to find an excuse to spend more time with you."

She considers this, then says, "Can I be honest with you?"

"Yeah."

"I didn't want you to take me home this afternoon."

I feel the surprise on my face, followed by notable relief.

She smiles at me.

And I smile back.

WE LEAVE BRIDGEWATER and travel back down the lake at a much slower pace than when we came up this afternoon. The night air has cooled considerably, and it's pleasant in comparison to the heat of the afternoon.

Carson is asleep on the back seat. Keegan is standing next to me, looking out at the dark in front of us as I drive.

"It's a lot trickier at night, isn't it?" she asks, raising her voice above the boat's motor.

"Especially if you don't know the lake," I say. "It can get confusing.

We're on a wide water stretch, and I note a mile marker as we pass it, double-checking that we're where I think we are.

"Thanks for the day, Bowie. It's been kind of perfect."

"I should thank *you*," I say. "And yeah, it has."

I glance at her for a second, see the look of sincerity on her face and think to myself that you really can't anticipate the sudden turns life can take. For good or bad. I know better than to try, but even so, the sound of a boat engine somewhere close, too close, catches me off guard.

I look quickly in either direction, but I don't see it until it is nearly on top of us. The boat has no lights on. We do.

Surely, the driver will see us. The worst kind of fear slams me hard in the chest. I hit the throttle, trying to get out of the way, yelling for Keegan to get down and hold on.

But it's too late because the driver doesn't see us. And there's no way to get out of the boat's path.

It sounds like a freight train is roaring down on us. And then the nose hits the back of our boat. Gravity disappears, and there is nothing to hold onto, just the night air and then cold, dark water swallowing us whole.

*

No one can confidently say that he will still be living tomorrow.
– Euripides

Keegan

IT'S LIKE A nightmare, the kind where you're almost awake but not quite enough to pull yourself back into the light.

But the water around me is real. And the realization that it is filling my lungs more real still. I grapple for the surface, fighting my way up, up until I break through, coughing and gasping for air.

I'm trying to figure out what has happened when I hear the screams. It's a man. Sounding as if he's in agony.

Terror yanks my heart into my throat.

Is it Bowie?

I feel water splashing near me, hear a whimper that I recognize as Carson. I kick my feet, dizzy but aware enough to swim toward the sound. "Here, Carson," I say.

I feel him bump against me, his paws latching onto my shoulders. He clings to me.

"It's okay," I say, kicking to stay afloat. "I've got you."

"Keegan!"

Now I hear Bowie. Thank God. "Here!" I call out.

Water splashes. The moaning sound from somewhere nearby continues, and I scream, "Bowie, are you all right?"

"Yes. Are you?"

"I think so. I have Carson. But someone else is hurt!"

"Stay where you are!" Bowie yells. "I'm coming."

I kick as hard as I can to stay afloat. Carson is holding onto me just like a person would, shaking so hard that I try to pull him closer to comfort him.

A full minute passes before Bowie reaches us. He immediately loops an arm around my waist to help hold me up. "Are you okay?"

"I think so," I say.

"Come here, boy," Bowie says, tucking his arm around Carson and saying, "Hold onto my shirt, Keegan. There's a little jut of land a hundred yards or so away. I'm going to get us there."

"I can swim," I say.

"I'm not letting go of you," he says, and I hear in his voice that he won't relent. "Hold on."

I do and then realize I no longer hear the moans from a minute before.

"Where are the people in the other boat, Bowie?" I scream out. "I don't hear anyone now."

"Keegan, don't let go," he says, and I can hear that he's out of breath.

"Are you hurt?"

"I'm okay," he says.

But somehow, I know he isn't.

Whosoever is spared personal pain
must feel himself called
to help in diminishing the pain of others.
– Albert Schweitzer

Bowie

WHEN I FINALLY REACH the small jut of land that is a high point in the middle of the lake, I have never been so grateful to touch ground. Rocks at the edge of the shoreline cut at my arms, but I don't care. I collapse onto them, not letting go of Keegan or Carson.

I struggle to sit up, still pulling in air. Carson tries to stand and staggers against me with a whimper. I hold onto his collar, running my hands across him.

"Keegan, are you okay?"

"I think so," she says. "My head hurts, but I don't think anything is broken."

I try to focus, but find that my thoughts don't want to stay in line. I blink hard and try to focus on the area where the boat hit us. "I can't see anything out there," I say. "Do you see anyone?"

"I heard someone," Keegan says, her voice shaking. "But I don't now."

"Is anyone out there?" I call out. "Anyone out there?" But there's no answer, and I don't want to think about what that might mean.

"We need help," Keegan says.

"Someone will come along soon. This part of the lake gets a lot of traffic."

"Even this late?" she asks, tears in her voice again. "Those people out there, the ones in the other boat—"

"Don't," I say, touching her arm. "It came out of nowhere, Keegan. There was nothing we could do."

"I never saw it," she agrees. "Did the boat have lights on?"

I shake my head. "No," I say. "I saw it right before it hit us."

I'm feeling dizzy again, and I wonder if I've missed something. I check my arms, my torso, and then my legs. That's when I see the gash on my thigh. There's blood oozing from the tear in my shorts. A lot of blood now that the water isn't diluting it.

"Oh, no, Bowie," Keegan says, spotting the wound at the same time. "You're hurt!"

"It's just a cut," I say.

"But there's so much blood. And we don't know how much you've already lost."

I start to protest, but my vision funnels, dark and then widening with a beckoning light. I try to tell her I'm okay, but I can't make the words come out. And then I fall headfirst into the funnel, unable to stop myself.

*

He who has a why to live can bear almost any how.
– Friedrich Nietzsche

Keegan

I START TO SCREAM his name over and over again. I shake his shoulders, but he has dropped back onto the shore as if all the life has drained from him. I'm still screaming when I check the pulse in his neck, feeling it there, faint, but there.

"Bowie!" I keep saying his name, trying to think what to do. The bleeding. I have to stop the bleeding. I try to remember anything I've ever learned about first aid, ripping my blouse open, the buttons popping off. I struggle out of it, glad I'm also wearing a camisole. I frantically try to figure which way to tear it that will allow for fabric long enough to wrap around Bowie's leg as a tourniquet.

At first the fabric doesn't want to give, and I scream in frustration. Carson huddles against me, shivering. I modulate my voice, telling him it's okay. He whimpers in a way that ties a knot in my heart, and I know he must realize that Bowie is hurt.

"We're going to help him," I say. The fabric finally gives, and I'm able to tear a strip long enough and wide enough to do the job. I shove Bowie's shorts up high enough on his leg to get the tourniquet in place. The sight of the wound makes my stomach leap with fear. I know that this will only help for so long. The gash is deep, and I don't know if it has hit a major artery.

I tie the tourniquet as tight as I dare, staring at the wound while I pray that the bleeding will at least slow, if not stop altogether. A minute or more passes before it does slow, the gash leaking in a trickle instead of a steady flow.

And then I start to pray that someone will come along and find us. Soon.

I DON'T KNOW HOW long it actually is before a boat light appears against the unrelenting black of the night. I see the red and green lights before I hear the boat's engine.

I'm shivering as I jump to my feet, waving and screaming with everything I have inside me. Carson starts barking, as if he knows this is how he can help.

I am sure the boat is going to fly on by without seeing us, because it passes the little island where we are without slowing down. But then, the driver pulls the throttle back completely, the boat coming to an abrupt stop, bobbing high on the waves it's created.

I begin screaming for help again.

"Where are you?" a man's voice calls out urgently.

"On the little jut of land to your right," I call back. "We were hit by another boat. My friend is hurt. He's bleeding a lot. I don't know what happened to whomever was on the other boat."

I can't go on then, because I'm crying at the thought that we have heard no other voices since right after the impact.

"I'm calling 911!" the driver says. "I'll be right over there. Stay put, okay?"

"Yes," I say. "Yes."

THE DRIVER IS a retired police officer. He and his wife had been to dinner at Bridgewater, had in fact been eating at the pizza place when we were there.

He made arrangements with the 911 operator to meet the rescue squad at the marina. He could get us there far more quickly than waiting for them to get to us on the lake. The woman has given me her sweater to wear, and at least I am not shivering so violently now.

The ambulance arrives just seconds after the man pulls up to the main dock. His wife, a woman with white hair and a kind face, has been gripping my hand the entire time. "You poor thing," she says. "You must be in shock."

I'm not sure if I am or not, but something that feels like a protective shield has formed around my heart and brain, and I feel numb.

The paramedics run to the dock carrying two stretchers.

When they reach the boat, I say, "I'm okay. Please help Bowie. He's lost a lot of blood."

They do as I've asked, but as soon as they have him hooked up to an IV and have replaced my tourniquet with one of their own, the female paramedic starts attending to me.

I realize Carson won't be able to go with us in the ambulance, so I ask the couple who found us if they could please take him to my house. I borrow one of their phones and call Evan, getting his voicemail. I leave a message, telling him what has happened and asking him to meet the people at our dock, hoping he will get it before they arrive there.

I'm allowed to ride in the ambulance with Bowie. He is awake now, and so visibly in pain that I can hardly bear to look at him.

"Hang on, now," the paramedic says. "We're going to get you to the hospital just as fast as we can."

I've assured them that I'm fine, but I'm grateful for the huge blanket they wrap me in. Its warmth stops my teeth from chattering. I want to ask them if Bowie will be all right, but I'm afraid of their answer and don't want him to hear anything other than what's absolutely necessary.

The ride is winding, and even though the ambulance feels as though it is flying, siren screaming the entire way, it seems as if we will never get there. Time is lengthened by my fear for Bowie. I wonder if there is anyone I should call. But I don't know the answer to that, and since I don't have his cell phone, I have no way to figure that out.

We finally arrive at the hospital's emergency entrance. A doctor in a white coat meets us at the large glass door. The paramedics jump out of the vehicle, telling him quickly what Bowie's condition is. He glances at the wound on Bowie's leg and says in an urgent voice, "We need to get him to the OR, stat."

Three other members of the hospital staff run outside and begin following the doctor's orders to get Bowie inside and straight to the operating room.

I hear in his voice that this is serious. I can't believe this has happened. It all seems suddenly surreal, as if I am in the middle of a nightmare, at the part where I'm trying to wake up but can't quite get there.

I feel lightheaded, as if all the oxygen has just been sucked from my lungs. I reach for something to grab onto, but there isn't anything, and I'm falling. Back, back, down.

*

Realization is a slow dawn.
– Author Unknown

Evan

I'M DRIVING mom's car as fast as I dare. I know I'm breaking the speed limit, but all I can think is that I have to get to the hospital.

I think about the solemn-faced man and woman who had shown up at the door with Carson and explained to me what had happened. At first, I just stared at them, sure that I was being punked or the butt of some crappy joke.

But their expressions of sympathy had not changed, and they'd asked if there was anything else they could do for me. I thanked them, realizing in a burst of panic that I had to go. I dried Carson off as much as I could, gave him a water bowl and showed him where the couch was, hoping he would make use of it.

All I can think about now is what Analise had said this afternoon. About realizing almost too late what her dad really meant to her. I must have sounded like an arrogant jerk, questioning her, and maybe in some way implying that she shouldn't have felt like that.

And now I get it.

You can in no way imagine what something will be like until it actually happens to you. The couple who brought

Carson to the house told me that Mom seemed okay. But Bowie was hurt. What if they were wrong about Mom?

Another boat ran full speed into them. It's hard to believe they're alive. And the people in the other boat . . . apparently no one could find them.

I slow the Rover for a sharp turn, accelerating quickly when it straightens out.

I need to get there. *Please let her be all right. Please. Let her be all right.*

*

Sometimes things fall apart so that better things can fall together.
– Marilyn Monroe

Bowie

MY AWARENESS comes and goes.

I know my situation is now urgent. I can tell by the rush of the people pushing this gurney, by the low, serious intonation in their voices.

I have the sense that we're on an elevator. And then we're off. A female voice is calling my name. Mr. Dare. Mr. Dare.

I try to force my eyes open, but it's starting to feel as if someone has wired them shut. I can't make them open. I want to answer her. I want to know how bad this is. What they're going to do.

I hear a man's voice say, "Get him to the OR. We don't have any time to waste."

I focus on that last word. Try to place its meaning. Waste. To fiddle away. When something is a shame.

Ah, I think. That's what this would be. A waste. Finding someone like Keegan. And never getting the chance to see where it might go. A waste. That would be a . . . waste.

*

Appreciation is an excellent thing. It makes what is excellent in others belong to us, as well.
– Voltaire

Keegan

I'M SITTING UP in the ER hospital bed, sipping orange juice when Evan throws back the curtain and says, "Mom!"

"Evan," I say, and then seeing the distress on his face, reach out my hand. "I'm okay."

He takes it, sitting on the side of the bed and putting his arms around me in a tight hug. "Are you sure?"

"Yes," I say. "I hope I didn't scare you too much."

"Actually, you did," he says, leaning back to look at me then.

I see the tears in his eyes, and they surprise me. I can't remember the last time I saw Evan cry and certainly not about anything related to me. I run my hand across his hair and say, "I'm sorry."

"I'm just glad to see you. I imagined everything."

"I should have tried to call you after we got here."

"It's okay. How is Bowie?"

The question brings up a fresh wave of fear inside me. "They haven't told me anything in a little while. They were taking him to surgery."

"What happened?"

"Another boat came out of nowhere and rammed into the back of ours. We were all thrown out. To be honest, I'm not sure how we're alive. Bowie managed to swim Carson and me to a little island not far from the wreck. When we got there, we realized he had a horrible wound on his leg."

Evan's face gets pale. "He was bleeding that whole time?"

I nod, feeling sick again at the thought. "Yes. I don't know how he did that. I think he was just so determined to get us to safety."

"What about the other people?"

A fresh wave of sadness hits me. "I heard someone screaming right after the crash. But then nothing after that."

Evan shakes his head. "I can't believe it. How could that have happened?"

"I don't know, Ev. It was horrible. Really."

He pulls me back to him again, hugging me hard. "I'm sorry for being such a jerk all the time, Mom."

"It's your job," I say. "You're seventeen."

I feel him smile against my hair. "I'm going to do better," he says.

"You're doing fine," I say.

"Want me to go see if I can find out anything about Bowie?"

"Would you, please?"

"Yeah. I'll be right back, okay?"

I nod, watching him go, praying that he will come back with good news.

Although the world is full of suffering, it is full also of the overcoming of it.

– Helen Keller

Bowie

I FEEL A STAB of pain so deep, so intense that I sit straight up. It is as if it has seared every bone in my body. I want to yell, beg it to stop, but I can't push the words out. It's like I'm trapped inside it. Above it. Below it.

I hear an urgent voice. "Heart rate elevating!"

Am I awake? Am I dead?

I feel myself falling. And as I go, the pain goes too.

*

Some choices do not come with the opportunity to be undone.
– Author Unknown

Keegan

WHEN EVAN COMES back fifteen minutes later, he is pale and subdued. "I couldn't get a lot of information because I'm not family. All they would tell me is that he's still in surgery."

"He's going to be all right. I can't let myself think anything other than that," I say.

"I know. He's a tough guy."

But it's clear that we're both worried, both scared for him.

"I did hear one of the nurses talking about the accident. There were two people on the other boat. A man and a woman. They still haven't found them yet. Divers are going to start looking in the morning."

The words are shocking. I feel the brunt of them like blows from a mallet. "Oh, no," I say. "That's so horrible."

"She said someone had seen them at a bar on the lake earlier tonight. They were both pretty hammered."

I shake my head at the senselessness of it. But I feel no anger. Just pity and sorrow that it had cost them their lives.

*

Let us cross over the river and rest under the shade of the trees.

– Thomas Stonewall Jackson

Bowie

THE VOICE IS TELLING me to wake up. "We need to know you're with us, Mr. Dare. Come on now. Time to be awake."

My eyelids feel as if they are weighted with boulders. Pushing them open feels like it will take a feat of strength I am not capable of.

But the voice continues to prod. So I continue to try. Until finally, light appears in the slit of my eyelids.

"That's it. Keep going. You're getting here."

I try to say something, but my lips are so dry I can't force words past them. I struggle to find the person attached to the voice. Her face appears before me, hazy and indistinguishable at first.

"There you are," she says. "Back where you're supposed to be." She puts her hand over mine. "You're going to be fine, Mr. Dare. You've had quite a night, but you're going to be fine."

There's something I want to ask her, but the question won't come to me. I grasp at it, like a child grabbing at snowflakes only to find they instantly melt and disappear.

Sleep pulls hard at me again, and just before I let it lull me back under, the question comes to me. Keegan and Carson. Are they okay?

*

Children are great imitators. So give them something great to imitate.
– Anonymous

Keegan

I END UP staying in the hospital overnight. My blood pressure is low, and the attending ER doctor said he wanted to err on the side of caution. And besides, he'd added with a grin, "You'll give the nurses conversation for the next week. Half of them are *Aimless* addicts."

Evan was allowed to stay in the room with me, even though it was against regular policy. I think the nurse who had brought me to my room felt sorry for him and didn't want to be responsible for sending him home when he clearly wanted to be with me a while longer.

He wakes up not too long after I do. He stretches his long body and says, "I don't care what they say, this is not a sleeping chair."

"You looked a bit like a pretzel there."

"I feel like one."

A nurse walks in just then, carrying a tray of breakfast. I thank her for it and then ask, "Is there any way I can find out how Bowie Dare is doing. He went for surgery last night when we were both brought in."

The nurse, a young woman who couldn't be too long out of nursing school smiles at me and says, "I'll go check. Be right back."

True to her word, she returns in a couple of minutes, her voice low when she says, "I called upstairs to ask about him. He's out of surgery and apparently is in stable condition."

The relief hits me in such a wave that I drop back against the pillows, tears instantly welling in my eyes. "Oh, thank goodness. I've been so worried about him."

"I'm glad I could let you know then, Ms. Monroe. Is there anything else I can get for you?"

"No. And thank you so much."

She turns to leave the room, hesitating at the door and saying, "It's really cool to meet you. I have been such a fan of your show."

"That's nice to hear. Thank you so much."

She's gone then. I glance at Evan, expecting to see the boredom I've grown used to seeing there when someone mentions my work in front of him. But it's not boredom I see there now. It's something more like pride, and it's kind of unbelievable how nice that feels.

*

A man who dares to waste one hour of time has not discovered the value of life.
– Charles Darwin

Bowie

I DON'T REALLY know why I'm surprised to see her, but I am.

Keegan stands in the doorway to my room, smiling as if she couldn't be happier to see me. "Hey," she says.

"Hey," I say, my voice still raspy from the aftereffects of the anesthesia.

"You have no idea how good it is to set eyes on you," she says, walking over to the bed and sitting on the chair beside me.

"Are you okay?" I ask, even though I can see that she appears to be.

"I'm fine."

"And Carson?"

"He's at my house. The couple who helped us last night took him there after we met the rescue squad. Evan just left to go home and feed him and take him out."

"Thank you," I say, hearing the relief in my voice.

We stare at each other for a few moments, and I have to think we're feeling a lot of the same things. Gratitude. Awareness that we might very well have not been alive this morning.

"One of the nurses told me about the people in the other

boat," I say. "I asked and she didn't really want to tell me, but I think I already knew."

"It's so sad," Keegan says.

"It is. I wish I could have done something—"

"You did," she says. "You saved our lives. I wish we could have helped them too. But it wasn't possible. And I will never understand how you swam all that way, pulling Carson and me when you had that awful injury to your leg."

"I never felt it until we stopped."

"Thank you," she says. "For what you did for me last night."

"Actually, I think I'm the one who should be thanking you. The surgeon told me that your tourniquet for sure saved my life."

"I was so scared I'd do something wrong. I'm glad I didn't."

We watch each other for a few moments, something real and amazing settling between us. There's something about sharing life-changing experiences with another person that forever transforms what's between you. I think about the two fairly carefree people who had played putt-putt together last night. And the two people we are this morning.

I'm not sure where we go from here. I just know that I have never been more grateful to be alive.

*

Goodness is the only investment that never fails.
– Henry David Thoreau

Evan

ANALISE CALLS AS I'm driving back to the lake from the hospital.

"Is it true about your mom and Mr. Dare?" she asks when I pick up.

"Yeah," I say. "They're both okay. But it was pretty scary."

"I heard about it at the marina a few minutes ago. I'm so sorry, Evan. Is there anything I can do to help?"

"I think we're okay. I'm headed home for a bit to let Mr. Dare's dog out. He's at our house."

"Want to pick me up on the way? I'll be happy to keep you company."

When I don't answer right away, she says, "I mean, if not, that's okay."

"I'd like that, Analise," I say, realizing how much I'd like to have her with me right now.

"Okay," she says, sounding pleased. "I'll be waiting."

"See you in a few."

"Great."

"Hey, Analise?"

"Yeah?"

"You know what you said yesterday about not waiting until it's too late?"

"Yeah," she says softly.

"You were right," I say.

*

Love unlocks doors and opens windows that weren't even there before.

– Mignon McLaughlin

Keegan

A DOCTOR RELEASES me just before eleven. I'm waiting for Evan to come back and pick me up, so I return to Bowie's room to check in on him again.

He's staring out the window when I walk over to his bed. "Hi."

He glances at me as if I have surprised him. "Sorry," he says. "Little lost there."

"How are you feeling?"

"My leg hurts a bit, but not too bad."

"Do you know how long you'll have to be here?"

"The doctor said a couple of days. I guess infection is a concern. I'll be on IV antibiotics for a bit."

"Oh. That's good. I mean better to be cautious."

"Yeah. Would it be too much of an imposition to ask if Carson can stay with you until I'm released?"

"Of course not. Is there a particular kind of food I should get him?"

"You could go by my house and pick up some."

"Sure. How do I get in?"

He tells me where a key is hidden outside the house, then says, "Are you headed home now?"

"Just waiting on Evan to get back."

We're both awkward, as if we don't know what to say to each other. I finally say, "Are you all right, Bowie? I mean other than the obvious."

"Yeah," he says, and then adds, "Something weird happened during the surgery though."

"What?" I ask, sitting down on the side of the bed and noticing the unsettled look in his eyes.

"I think I woke up while they were working on my leg."

"What do you mean?" I ask, unable to hide my horror.

"I could hear the doctors talking. I could feel the sensation of what they were doing but no pain. I couldn't move though, couldn't tell them I was awake. It was as if I was paralyzed."

"Bowie." I put my hand on his, pressing hard. "That's horrible."

"I haven't been able to stop thinking about it. It was like I was trapped in my own body."

"Did you tell the doctors after you woke up?"

"I did, actually. The anesthesiologist said it's called 'accidental awareness during general anesthesia.'"

"Is this something that happens often?"

He shrugs a little. "He said maybe 1 in 20,000 patients."

"I've never heard of such a thing. I'm sorry, Bowie—"

"It's okay. I'm okay. It's just strange. I still have this panicky feeling. Like I'm trapped and trying to get out of a place I can't escape."

"Did you try to let them know you were awake?"

"I tried to move my hands and feet, to slide off the operating table. But I couldn't make myself move at all. It felt like I was dying."

I lean in then and put my arms around him, wanting to erase that incredibly dreadful feeling. "That's a terrible thing to go through."

"Not something I ever imagined experiencing."

I squeeze his hand, wishing I had some other comfort to offer. But this seems like one that only time will make fade. "Is there anything I can do?"

"No. It should give me something to write about anyway."

"Maybe a horror novel."

"Yeah." I glance out the window and then back at him. "I can't stop thinking about last night. I've never been involved in anything where someone actually died. Those poor people."

"I've been thinking about it too."

"I guess it's not a first for you, considering the work you did."

"No. But it never gets easier to handle."

"I still hear his voice in my head. Calling for help."

"I wish we could have gotten to him."

"Did you hear the woman?'

"No."

"I hope that means she never suffered."

"There wasn't anything we could do, Keegan. You have to let yourself believe that."

"Logically, I know that. But the whole thing kind of feels like a nightmare. I woke up this morning, feeling for a second as though it might have been a dream and never happened."

"Hey."

I look up to find Evan standing in the doorway. I let go of Bowie's hand as if we've just been caught making out in the living room. "Hey. You're back fast."

"Figured you'd be ready to get home."

This is the first time I've heard him refer to our new house as home. It feels nice to hear it. "That does sound good. I wish Bowie didn't have to stay."

"I'll be fine," Bowie says. "And thank you for taking care of Carson."

"Not a problem," Evan says. "He was snoozing on the couch when I left. And it's pretty cool that Mom doesn't seem to be scared of him. By the way, can I get a dog now, Mom?"

"You might make an excellent attorney," I say.

"He does have a knack for finding an angle," Bowie says, smiling a little.

Evan shrugs. "You take the opening when you see it."

I get up from the side of the bed and look at Bowie. "I do feel guilty leaving you here."

"Not to worry. I'm good."

"We'll check in on you later then," I say. "See ya'."

"See ya'," he says.

"YOU REALLY LIKE him, don't you?"

Evan asks the question once we're back in Franklin County, headed toward the lake. He's driving, and I've been resting in the passenger seat with my eyes closed.

"Who?" I ask, even though I know who he's talking about.

"Bowie."

"He's a good friend. A good neighbor."

"And that's all?" he asks, sounding skeptical.

"Evan, we barely know each other."

"Yeah, but I know how you usually are with men."

"Oh, you do?"

"I do. Ninety-eight percent of them don't pass the care-to-spend-time-with-you mark. And the other two percent rarely make it to a second date."

"I can't deny any of that. I learned a long time ago that it's much easier to never open a door in the first place than it is to close it when something doesn't work out."

"Seems like you've opened the door."

"Maybe just a crack."

Evan looks over at me. "I'm glad. You need someone nice in your life."

I hear a maturity in my son's voice that I've never before heard. It makes me at once happy and sad. "You're growing up, you know that?"

"Don't let the exterior fool you," he says, teasing.

"I won't," I say.

He reaches over and puts his hand over mine. "I'm really glad you're all right, Mom."

I try to answer him, but I can't seem to get any words out. I squeeze his hand back and look out the window instead.

*

The first step toward change is awareness. The second step is acceptance.
– Nathaniel Branden

Bowie

I TRY TO TELL her I'll get another way home, but Keegan insists on picking me up when I'm released from the hospital. A nurse wheels me outside to meet her just before noon, three days after the accident.

"I'm sure you're ready to go home," she says, just as Keegan pulls up to the entrance.

"Yes," I say.

"And your wife is right on time to get you," she says.

I don't bother to correct her because I don't want to extend my stay even for the duration of a conversation. I've never been fond of hospitals, thankful for the good they do, but ready to not be here.

She opens the Range Rover door for me. I stand up from the wheelchair, not putting weight on my right leg but still managing to shift into the passenger seat.

"Thank you," I say.

"Take care, now," the nurse says and shuts the door.

"Hey," Keegan says, looking at me with a smile. "You look like yourself now."

I laugh and say, "Glad to hear it."

"Your color is back and everything," she says by way of explanation.

"I feel like myself too," I say. "Just glad to be leaving that place. The thing about a hospital is the longer you stay, the sicker you start to think you are."

"That experience when you were in the OR, it shook you up, didn't it?"

I glance out the window, considering my answer. "Maybe everyone has a deep down fear of something. Mine is being trapped in a place I can't get out of. My work started to feel like that at some point. But I never imagined being trapped inside my own body."

She reaches over and puts her hand on my arm, as if to remind me I'm here and not there.

"The funny thing is I think it reminded me of how claustrophobic my old life was. And how glad I am to have the life I have now. Simple as it is."

I feel Keegan studying me and let myself meet her gaze.

"I'm beginning to really appreciate simple," she says.

We don't hurry to look away from each other. I see in her eyes awareness of a shared experience that will forever bond us whether we continue to know each other or not.

"Anywhere you need to go?" she asks in a soft voice.

"I could use a new phone. Do you have time to stop?"

"I booked you for the entire day," she says. "Where to?"

WITHIN AN HOUR, I have a new phone. Keegan ended up replacing hers at the same store, creating a new contract with a local number. One of the employees recognizes her, and a small circle of customers and store workers gather around to ask for her autograph. I stand back and watch how she treats them like old acquaintances, answering questions about the show and whether it will continue on without her.

We're headed back to the lake when she says, "Sorry about that."

"The fan stuff?"

She nods.

"I like watching you in action."

She smiles and says, "What do you mean?"

"You're just kind to people."

She focuses on the road ahead for a moment, then says, "I'd really rather have that said about me, more than just about anything."

"It's true."

"I don't think I always was. In the beginning."

"Of your career?"

She nods. "I had a lot of anger. I'm afraid I misdirected it for a while."

"We're all a work in progress," I say. "Seems like you figured it out."

"Thanks," she says, and I can tell she really means it. "Carson misses you terribly by the way."

"I've missed him."

"He's really good company," she says. "Evan has been seeing Analise a lot, so it's just been the two of us hanging out at the house."

"I hope it wasn't too much of an imposition."

"I've actually loved having him around. In fact, I was

wondering if you might be willing to go with me to pick out a dog at the local shelter. When you're feeling better, I mean. Evan has wanted one forever, and I—"

"I'd be really happy to do that," I say. "Any time you want to."

"Thanks," she says, glancing over to meet eyes with me. "Would you be up for it tomorrow?"

"Tomorrow, it is."

We can do no great things, only small things with great love.

– Mother Teresa

Keegan

I DECIDE NOT TO tell Evan that we're going. If for some reason, it doesn't work out, I don't want him to be disappointed.

Bowie insists on driving, even though I know his leg must be sore. "There's a county shelter about forty minutes away where the dogs don't always get out," he says. "Is that the kind of place you want to go to?"

"What do you mean?" I ask. "Don't always get out?"

"They have a limited time to be adopted."

"Or they're put to sleep?"

He nods, his expression regretful. "It's not easy to go there, but you'll definitely be saving a life."

I consider this, nodding, not sure how I feel about going into such a place. "Yes. Okay."

Bowie brings Carson along, and he rides in the seat between us, curling up immediately for a nap.

Bowie and I make small talk all the way to the shelter. We both seem reluctant to touch on anything too significant, and I find myself feeling nervous about what I'm about to do. What if I can't choose?

By the time Bowie pulls the truck into the gravel parking lot in front of a small brick building, I actually feel sick with nerves. He gets out, telling Carson to stay. I open my door and slide out.

"You're sure you want to do this?" Bowie asks, looking at me with concern in his eyes. "We can go somewhere else if you'd rather. There's an adoption center—"

"No," I say. "This is good. Let's go in."

He leads the way, and I follow him up the short stairs and through the main door. A woman with curly hair and round glasses looks up from the front desk.

"Can I help you?" she asks.

"I'm interested in adopting a dog," I say.

"What kind?"

"I'm not sure."

"If you can give me an idea what you're looking for," she says, looking irritated, "I can tell you if we have anything like that. You want an urgent status dog, or does that matter?"

"Urgent status?" I repeat.

"Meaning their time is up," she says, as if speaking to someone incapable of understanding her words. "And today will be their last day. Before they're euthanized."

"I—how many are urgent status?"

"Two."

"Keegan," Bowie says, sympathy in his voice. "We can go if—"

"May I see them?" I ask.

"I'll have to bring them out here. Visitors aren't allowed in the kennels."

"Okay," I say, wondering suddenly if I should have just asked her to bring out one of them. How can I possibly choose between them?

Bowie and I wait in silence until she disappears through a heavy metal door.

"Are you sure this is what you want—" Bowie begins.

"Yes," I say, even though I'm not sure at all. I just know I can't leave.

She's back in a couple of minutes, pushing through the door as if she has far more pressing things to do than bring out dogs for me to look at. My gaze snags on the puppy under her left arm. A tiny black and tan face stares back at me, eyes wide with concern.

My heart takes an instant nose dive. "Ohhh," I say.

"This one," she says, tipping her head at the puppy in her arms. "And this one."

I follow her gaze then to the dog following behind her on a nylon leash.

"Although I'm sure you'll be taking the puppy," the woman says.

The dog now standing beside her looks as if he knows she's right. His posture is dejected and tired. His black coat is matted in places, and he's clearly in need of a bath. His ears are gray at the tips, and his muzzle has started to whiten. His tail is tucked between his legs, and I'm fairly certain he doesn't expect another good thing to ever happen for him.

I know that feeling. Early in my life, those were my own expectations.

I glance at the puppy and then back at the dog. "I'll take them," I say.

"Both?" the woman asks, surprise in her voice, and then a grudging respect, when she adds, "You're sure?"

"Yes. I want them both."

*

I am only one, but I am one. I cannot do everything, but I can do something. And I will not let what I cannot do interfere with what I can do.

– Edward Everett Hale

Bowie

CARSON GIVES BOTH dogs a thorough inspection outside the truck before giving the tail-wag okay for me to let them in. He rides up front with me, and Keegan gets in the back seat with the puppy and the old guy, insisting that's where she wants to be.

We're pulling out of the parking lot when Keegan finds my gaze in the rearview mirror. "You think I'm nuts, don't you?"

"I don't think that at all. I just hope you didn't feel pressured to take them both. I'll feel bad if you regret it."

"I won't," she says, and I can hear in her voice that it's true. "I never knew it was like that."

"The limited time to be adopted?"

"Yes," she says. "It's so horrible."

I glance at the puppy curled up in her lap. And the old dog with his head resting on her thigh. "It is horrible."

"What about tomorrow and the ones who are 'urgent status' then? What if no one comes for them?" she asks, tears in her voice.

"You have to think about the ones you've helped," I say. "You can't let yourself think beyond that."

But she's quiet the rest of the drive home. And I know she's clearly thinking about it.

Love begins at home, and it is not how much we do... but how much love we put in that action.
– Mother Teresa

Keegan

AS SOON WE get back to the house, I decide to give them each a bath. There's a shower in the bathroom next to the pool, and that seems like a good place to do it.

Bowie waits outside with them while I run in and change into shorts and a T-shirt, grabbing a big bottle of shampoo and conditioner from my bathroom.

Carson is playing with the puppy when I get back, so I decide to start with the older guy. He looks unsure, but I think he's already decided I'm trustworthy because he follows me into the bathroom and walks into the shower stall as if he's done it a hundred times.

I let the water get warm and use the shower spray to soak his coat. Reddish dirt streams from it, and I wonder when he last had a bath. He closes his eyes and stands quietly, as if it feels like heaven to him. I lather him up with my good shampoo, scrubbing his skin until there's no sign of dirt at all.

I then rinse him thoroughly, standing back to give him an admiring appraisal. "You look amazing," I say.

He wags his tail, swishing water.

Bowie comes in the bathroom, holding the puppy. "You ready for this little girl?"

"Trade you," I say.

"Thought of names yet?" he asks.

"Maybe Noah for this fellow," I say. "And Molly for this sweetie."

"Noah and Molly it is," he says.

I take the puppy from him and Noah walks out of the shower. Bowie calls him, and they head back to the pool.

Molly takes no time at all to get clean. She wags her little tail and tries to entice me to play as I rub the shampoo into her coat, smiling at her puppy growls.

Both dogs seem as if they have come to life in the past two hours. Somehow, they had known they weren't in a good place. I think they feel safe again. And for the first time in a really long time, I feel like I've done something that actually matters.

THE LOOK ON Evan's face when he arrives home later in the afternoon to find Noah and Molly playing on our kitchen floor is pretty much priceless.

"Are they ours?" he asks, looking at me as if he's not sure he recognizes me.

"They are," I say. "Meet Noah, the big guy. And Molly is the puppy."

He walks over and drops down on his knees next to Noah, reaching out to rub under his chin. "How did you—"

"Bowie took me to the shelter this afternoon."

"And you actually decided to adopt two?" he asks, incredulous.

"They both needed us," I say, deciding not to elaborate beyond that.

"Mom. That's amazing."

Molly crawls onto his lap, planting her tiny paws on his chest and trying to lick his face. Evan laughs and lifts her up.

"What made you decide to do this?" he asks.

"We need some more love in this house, don't you think?"

"Yeah," he says, looking at me with a smile. " I guess you can never have too much of that."

SEEING THE WAY Evan interacts with Noah and Molly makes me realize how good their company will be for him.

He spends hours on the living room floor with them, playing with Molly and just hanging out with Noah. He takes them both outside numerous times to get them used to going potty in a certain area.

Bowie calls after dinner to see how we're doing.

"They're amazing," I say. "I wish I'd done this sooner. I wish I had known—"

"I think you did it right when you needed to. And right when they needed you. Doesn't get much better than that."

"Thanks," I say. "For taking me there today. And for being such a good friend."

"You're welcome," he says. "I was glad to be a part of it."

We're quiet for several moments. I think about the fact that I've thanked him for being a good friend. And I know as surely as I've ever known anything that I want him to be more than that. I want us to be more than that.

But I don't know how to say it. Or maybe I'm just scared to.

"All right then," he says. "Have a good night, Keegan."

"You too, Bowie."

And we hang up without me saying anything at all.

*

Why not go out on a limb? That's where the fruit is.
– Mark Twain

Bowie

TWO WEEKS PASS, and I barely see Keegan or Evan. She calls to check on my leg a few times, but we don't make any plans to see each other. It's like we've both realized the feelings getting a foothold between us would have shallow roots at best, with no real chance of becoming anything permanent.

I bury myself in the book I'm working on, starting early and finishing late. I set personal records for daily word count. Losing myself in the story keeps me from picking up the phone and dialing Keegan's number against my better instincts.

That doesn't mean I don't think about her.

I do.

I run into Evan one afternoon at the marina when I stop in for gas. I'm driving the new boat I bought after mine was declared not worth fixing.

Evan is driving a new Mastercraft with big speakers on the tower. Noah is sitting on the seat beside him, looking as if he's been a lake dog his whole life.

Carson jumps out of my boat and trots over to greet them, wagging his tail.

"Hey, Evan," I say, following Carson.

"Hey, Bowie," Evan says. "It's good to see you. How's your leg?"

"Pretty much healed," I say.

"That's great to hear," he says.

"Like the new ride."

"Yeah, Mom got cool points for this one."

"I'm sure you're doing some good skiing behind that."

"I'm still not very good, but it makes me look better than I am."

I smile at that. "How're the pups?" I ask, reaching over to rub Noah's head.

"Awesome. Molly's with Mom. She's not as crazy about the boat as Noah is."

"How is your mom?" I ask, trying to sound nonchalant.

"Good," he says, and then, hesitating, adds, "Why'd you two stop hanging out?"

The question surprises me, and I'm not sure how to answer honestly without sounding like a loser. "Ah, you know, I'm sure a woman like your mom has hotter irons in the fire."

"If she does, she's not interested in any of them," Evan says, looking at me directly. "Can I be honest with you?"

"Yeah," I say. "Sure."

"She likes you. A lot. And I can tell she wondered why you quit calling."

"It wasn't really like that, Evan."

"Hey, I get it. Because she's a celebrity, you think you'd be a temporary thing. I wouldn't want to be that either. But I know my mom. And she likes you. She hasn't really liked a guy for a long time. It'd be nice if you called her. I'm pretty sure she's kind of lonely."

It's clear that Evan has gone out on a limb here. And I'm sure Keegan wouldn't want him disclosing all of this to me.

But I can tell that he loves his mom. And wants to see her happy. "I'd like to see her, Evan. I'll call her."

"Cool," he says, nodding. "Just don't tell her—"

"I won't," I say.

Footsteps sound on the dock behind us. I glance over my shoulder to see Analise jogging toward us in shorts and a bathing-suit top. "Hey," she says to both of us.

"Hey, yourself," Evan says, making an obviously deliberate effort to keep his gaze on her face. "Ready to ski?"

"Ready to show you how," she teases.

"I'd like to deny it," Evan says, looking at me. "But she smokes me."

"You two have fun out there. Be careful."

THE FOURTH OF JULY is only two days away, so I decide to ask Keegan if she would like to come over for dinner and watch the fireworks from my dock.

I'm actually nervous dialing her number.

She answers on the first ring. "Hey, Bowie."

"Hey," I say. "How are you?"

"Good. How's your leg?"

"Great. I saw Evan at the marina a couple days ago."

"He mentioned that," she says, sounding as if she's not sure where to go from there.

"I'd like to see you, Keegan."

"You would?"

Her surprise is clear, and that surprises me. "Yeah. I would. Would you like to come over for dinner on the fourth? There's always a big fireworks display on the lake after dark. I have a really good view from the dock here."

"I would love that," she says. "Can I bring something?"

"The dogs if you'd like, although I usually leave Carson in the house when the fireworks start going off. He gets pretty scared."

"I didn't think about that," she says. "Thanks for mentioning it."

"Seven o'clock sound good?"

"It does."

"I'll see you then."

"Hey, Bowie?"

"Yeah?"

"It's good to hear from you."

Secrets are things we give to others to keep for us.
– Elbert Hubbard

Keegan

I SIT WITH THE phone in my hand for a long while after Bowie and I hang up. Noah hops down from the couch, walks over and puts his head on my leg, as if he knows I'm thinking about something that needs his sympathy. Molly is stretched out on the floor, fast asleep with puppy exhaustion.

I rub Noah's head and say, "Well, that was a surprise."

He sits, his tail swishing across the floor.

"A good surprise. Do you think Evan had anything to do with that?"

Noah looks off, no longer wagging his tail.

"Oh, he told you to keep it a secret, did he?" I scratch under his chin. "I respect that. What do you think I should wear?"

He looks back at me, and I laugh because the look on his face is exactly what Evan's would be. *Seriously, Mom?*

*

Faith consists in believing when it is beyond the power of reason to believe. It is not enough that a thing be possible for it to be believed.

– Voltaire

Keegan

I FEEL AS IF I'm going on a first date.

It's ridiculous how nervous I am. I ask for Evan's approval on my outfit, and he gives me the same look Noah had given me, but does manage to add, "Yeah, that looks great, Mom."

I give the sleeveless summery dress a last look in the full-length mirror inside the downstairs half-bath. And then tell myself it is what it is.

In the living room, Evan is playing a video game.

"So Analise is coming over here?" I ask.

"Yeah. She's bringing pizza and a couple of friends with her."

"And you're planning to behave, right?"

"Mom."

"Evan."

"Yes, I'm planning to behave. Are you?" he asks, giving me a pointed look.

"I always behave," I say.

"With guys you're not attracted to," he says.

"Evan."

"Are you denying it?" he asks, taking aim at something on the TV screen and blasting away.

Since I can't, I just say, "Come on, Noah, Molly. I'll be home early, Ev."

"Believe it when I see it," he calls out as I shut the door behind us.

*

Soul meets soul on lovers' lips.
– Percy Bysshe Shelley, *Prometheus Unbound*

Bowie

IT'S ALMOST DARK when we take our wine glasses down to the dock, pulling chairs to the edge, facing Smith Mountain where the fireworks should soon begin.

The dogs are in the house, snoozing in a connected huddle.

"That was an amazing meal," Keegan says, setting her glass down on the dock.

"Lasagna was my mom's specialty. Mine doesn't compare to hers but I like to make it because it makes me think of her and my dad. He loved her cooking."

"Tell me about them," she says.

"I lost them both about ten years ago. They had gone to New York City for a shopping trip before Christmas. They were on the subway headed back to their hotel when a man tried to rob the passengers. An undercover police officer was in the car and tried to stop him. The guy just started shooting. My parents and three other people were killed."

"Oh, Bowie," she says, looking at me with horror in her eyes. "I'm so sorry."

"They didn't deserve to die like that. No one does, but they were kind people. Tried to live right. Give back."

Keegan reaches over and covers my hand with hers. She

doesn't say anything, but she doesn't need to. I feel her sympathy.

"Do you have any siblings?"

"No. I was the only one."

"That has to make it a lot harder."

"It would be nice to have someone else who remembers them the way I remember them. To share memories with."

We're quiet for a good bit, and then I say, "I try not to lead with that when I talk about my parents. It's not what they would want to be remembered for. My dad loved this lake so much. He really wanted to retire here. I wish he'd had the chance to do that."

"I bet he'd like knowing that you're here."

"I think he would. He always wanted the place to stay in the family."

"It's nice that you have those kinds of roots. It's what I always wanted most. Having family. I wanted to give that to my own children."

"I know it's what you're giving Evan."

"I hope so."

"Have you heard from your daughter?"

She shakes her head, looking down at our joined hands. "Sometimes, I feel so worried about her I can hardly bear it."

I consider what I'm about to say because I don't want to overstep lines I'm not certain I should cross. But the pain in her voice prompts me to say, "I still have friends who could possibly help, Keegan. Do you want me to talk with someone about looking for her?"

"More than anything, I would like to say yes," she says. "But she's asked me to leave her alone."

"Maybe you just need to know she's okay."

She meets my gaze then, and I see in her eyes how much she needs to know exactly that.

The first lights blast out against the black sky then.

"There they are," I say.

"Oh, wow," Keegan says. "It's beautiful."

The fireworks are an incredible display of color and sound. We sit, holding hands and watching the celebration for the next half hour or so.

When it's over, Keegan looks at me and says, "Can we sit out here for a while longer?"

"As long as you like," I say.

"May I ask you something, Bowie?"

"Sure," I say.

"Why isn't there anyone in your life? I mean, a man like you—"

She breaks off there, and while I could make light of the question, I decide that I owe her honesty. "I think I came to the conclusion at some point that being alone is better than being with the wrong person. Getting divorced was really awful."

"And you don't want to go through any of that again?"

"No," I say.

"Do you believe there's a right person and that it's just a matter of finding her?"

"I always have. I think I still do."

"But it's a risk."

"And Carson is pretty good company."

We both laugh, and then she says, "I'm not letting you off that easily though. You must get cakes and pies left at your door all the time."

"I could turn the tables and ask you the same question. Without the cakes and pies, of course."

She smiles.

"So why isn't there a man in your life?" I ask.

She looks out at the lake for a moment, as if considering her answer. "I've had serious boyfriends over the years, but honestly, it just became easier not to have anyone in my life. People usually bring a lot of baggage with them."

"Yeah. But if it's right, I guess their baggage should fit in the closet right next to your own."

"It should," she agrees.

"And then again, if it's right, it probably wouldn't matter if the fit was a little tight."

"Probably not."

We sit there for a good while, not saying anything further. Boats crisscross the lake, heading home after the fireworks display. A dog barks somewhere in the distance.

I look over at her, reaching for her hand. She slips it into mine, and I pull her up from her chair. We study each other, neither of us bothering to hide the longing that has been building between us.

She steps closer and places her hands on my chest, looking up at me, her lips parting slightly.

Without any more thought about what might happen beyond this moment, this night, I pull her to me, kissing her long and full and deep. Without letting fear of being hurt creep in and crowd out what feels utterly right and good.

And it is good. Kissing Keegan is like finding the purest spring water at the end of a mountain climb. I had no idea how much I needed this, needed her.

She kisses me back as if she needs me in the very same way. I feel the heat of her skin, run my hands through the silk of her hair.

"Should we go inside?" I ask against her ear.

"Yes, please," she says, urgency in the words.

I swing her up in my arms then, walking back to the house while she keeps kissing me.

"If I trip," I say, my voice uneven, "it will totally ruin the romance of this gesture."

She giggles, and I feel better once we only have the stretch of grass to cover.

Inside the house, I walk through the living room where all three dogs are curled up asleep on the couch, cracking an eye open to see what we're up to and then promptly ignoring us. I carry Keegan straight to my bedroom, pushing the door open with my shoulder and then kicking it closed behind us.

At the bed, I lower her carefully onto the mattress. She links her hands behind my neck and pulls me down beside her.

Everything goes a little crazy then. She's shoving my shirt off. I'm trying to unbutton her blouse. All the while, we're still kissing and exploring each other's body, heat and sweat and undeniable desire building between us.

A slice of moonlight slashes through the open curtains, and I stop for a moment to study the incredibly beautiful woman lying in my bed.

"You shouldn't be here," I say.

"Why?" she asks, sounding suddenly worried.

"Because you're too good to be true."

"I'm not, Bowie. I'm a regular girl who's found a guy she finds amazing. If you feel the same way about me, then let's just go with that. Okay?"

I could think of plenty of reasons to argue with her, insist that one of us is likely to end up regretting this. But I push all that aside, close out everything except what is right here, right now. This crazy-good feeling of having found something worth stepping out on the limb for. And it is. She is.

"Okay," I say and kiss her again.

*

But, instead of what our imagination makes us suppose and which we worthless try to discover, life gives us something that we could hardly imagine.
— Marcel Proust

Keegan

MY PHONE IS buzzing. It takes a moment for me to realize it's in the side pocket of my dress.

"Sorry," I say as Bowie reluctantly pulls his mouth from mine, his hand on my waist.

"Go ahead and get it," he says, his voice low and desire-filled.

"Just let me make sure it isn't Evan," I say, raising up on one elbow and squinting at the screen.

Reece's smiling face, along with her number, are all I can see. I fumble to pick it up, swiping the answer icon, and saying, "Reece? Are you there?"

There's no sound, and I'm terrified she's already hung up, but then I hear her crying. Soft and low as if she's trying to hide it but can't.

"Reece! Where are you? What's wrong?"

Bowie sits up in the bed beside me, a reassuring hand on my arm.

"Mom?"

Her voice is barely recognizable to me, weak and broken.

"Reece," I say, starting to cry now. "Tell me where you are."

"They took him," she says, adding something I can't understand.

"Who?" I manage, trying to keep myself together when it's all I can do not to sob. "Took who?"

"My baby," she finally says. "They took my baby."

*

Hope is patience with the lamp lit.
– Tertullian

Keegan

I TRY TO PROCESS what my daughter has just said to me. A dozen questions scramble together in my brain so that I can barely form one.

I'm sitting on the edge of the bed now, elbows on my knees, my head dropped forward in an attempt to ward off the dizziness swooping over me.

Bowie takes the phone from my hand, clicks on speaker phone and hands it back to me. I realize that he wants to hear the conversation in case he can help, and I'm swamped with sudden gratitude.

"Reece," I say. "Honey, please, slow down. Tell me what you're talking about."

"I just want him back," she says.

I hear the slurred edges of the words and feel panic hit the center of my chest. "Reece—"

Call failed flashes on the screen, and she is gone.

"Oh, no," I say, hitting the green call icon to try and get her back.

But the phone rings until her voice mail picks up. I try again with the same result.

I look at Bowie and start to cry. "She has a baby. She kept the baby."

Bowie pulls me to him. I press my face to his chest and sob. "What can I do?" I ask, feeling helpless as I have never before felt.

He leans back to look down at me, pushing my hair away from my face. "Let me make some calls. See if I can get a trace on her phone. We'll start from there. Okay?"

"Bowie. Oh, thank you. Thank you."

He pulls me to my feet, smoothing a gentle hand across my hair. "Don't worry," he says. "One step at a time."

I nod, biting my lip in an effort to hold back the sob at the back of my throat. I don't know what to think. What to feel. Until terror for my daughter rises above everything else. Terror for her and for a baby I never knew she had.

*

We secure our friends not by accepting favors but by doing them.
– Thucydides

Bowie

I START WITH Mitch Kane, my oldest friend in the bureau. We had worked together for a half-dozen years until he moved to an intelligence analyst position. I'm hoping he still has the connections to get me a trace on the call Reece just made.

I glance at the time, realizing it's almost midnight. Mitch answers with a groggy hello.

"Hey, Mitch. It's Bowie Dare."

"Bowie? Hey. Hold on a minute."

I hear a rustling noise, a door opening and closing, and then he's back with, "Hey, man. How are you?"

"Good, Mitch. Sorry to be calling you so late."

"Not a problem. What's up?"

"I have a friend whose daughter might be in trouble. And she just called her mom from a cell phone."

"Need a trace?"

"I'd owe you one."

"I don't think you'll ever owe me one, Bowie. You saved my life, remember?"

"Still. I wouldn't ask if it weren't important."

"I know that. Let me see what I can do. Give me the number."

Once he's jotted it down, I say, "Thanks, Mitch. I'll wait to hear from you. Hope I didn't wake Darla up."

"Aw, you know she's used to the phone ringing in the middle of the night. She's gotten really good at ignoring it."

"Tell her I said hello."

"I will, man. Check you in a bit."

I end the call, looking up to find Keegan standing in the office doorway.

"I hope it won't take long," I say.

"Thank you. I really don't know how to thank you."

I get up and walk over to her. "Are you okay?"

"I don't know what to think."

"Maybe you shouldn't. Let's just work on finding her first and then take it from there."

"I know you're right. I'm just imagining—"

"Don't," I say, rubbing my thumb across her cheek. "Just wait, okay?"

She closes her eyes and nods, saying, "I should call Evan."

"Go ahead," I say. "I'll let the dogs out."

"Thank you, Bowie. For everything. Thank you."

No one is useless in this world who lightens the burdens of another.

– Charles Dickens

Keegan

I HAD TOLD Evan I would wait at Bowie's until we heard back from his friend. It's almost two o'clock when Bowie's cell rings. We're in the kitchen, drinking coffee, and the sound of the phone vibrates through me like thunder.

Bowie answers, writing down what is being said to him on a yellow notepad. I sit on the barstool across from him, my hands clenched tightly together.

He speaks to the man on the other end for a minute or two, then puts down the phone and looks at me. "The call came from a residence in Knoxville, Tennessee."

"Knoxville?" I repeat. "Are you sure?"

He nods. "We can call the police there and ask them to check—"

"No," I say, becoming frantic. "I have to go there. I have to leave now."

"Keegan, wait. I'll drive you. By the time you get a flight, it would be faster to drive."

I want to tell him that's okay, that I'll go myself. But the thought of having him with me, drawing on his strength, is one I can't turn down. So I don't.

*

Let your advance worrying become advance thinking and planning.

– Winston Churchill

Bowie

WE DRIVE TO Keegan's house to leave the dogs with Evan. I wait outside while Keegan runs in to grab a few things from her room.

She's back in less than five minutes, jumping in the passenger seat of the Range Rover and insisting I drive.

"Is Evan okay?" I ask, backing out of the driveway and gunning down the road.

"He doesn't know what to make of the call any more than I do," she says. "He's worried about her. Bowie, what if she's—"

"Let's just get there as fast as we can," I say. "You try to sleep. I've got the driving."

She's quiet then, leaning back in her seat and staring out the window. I know she won't sleep. Fear won't let her. And so I do the only thing I know to do to help. Get her to her daughter as fast as possible.

*

Come away, O human child: To the waters and the wild with a fairy, hand in hand, For the world's more full of weeping than you can understand.
– William Butler Yeats

Keegan

IT'S BARELY SEVEN in the morning when we hit the outskirts of Knoxville. Bowie has keyed the address into his GPS. It's telling us we're ten minutes away from the location.

I'm so filled with anxiety that my chest feels tight with its inability to pull in air. Bowie reaches across and squeezes my hand, still saying nothing, because what is there to say?

I have no idea what we're going to find when we get there, and I can't let myself consider all the possibilities.

The GPS indicates we should take the next exit ahead. As soon as we reach the end of the ramp, it is apparent that the neighborhood is questionable at best.

"Go right and proceed three-quarters of a mile to destination," the GPS voice says.

Bowie does exactly that, slowing the vehicle to a stop in front of a very rundown two-story house that might have once been a nice home. Now, its paint is peeling in huge layers. Tiles hang from the roof and the window shutters lean drunkenly from their once-straight perch.

"This is horrible," I say. "She couldn't be in this place."

"You wait here," Bowie says. "I'll knock at the door."

"You don't have to do that," I start, but he stops me with a raised hand, indicating I should stay put.

I watch as he walks up the cracked concrete walkway and knocks at the door.

A full minute passes before the door opens a little more than an inch, and a young girl sticks her head out.

I watch Bowie talking to her, see her shake her head and try to shut the door. He stops her from closing it with one hand.

I can see her better now. She's dressed in torn jeans and a tattered T-shirt that is either brown or really dirty. Her teeth are the same brown as the shirt. I try to remember which drug has that effect on its users and come up with the word meth.

Bowie turns, waves for me to come to the door. All hope falls away then. Because I know she is here.

She's here.

*

The doors we open and close each day decide the lives we live.

– Flora Whittemore

Bowie

I WANT TO spare Keegan this. I've been in places like this before. I know what to expect. But I am sure that she does not. And I see that I'm right when the loaded young girl who had answered the door leads us to a room upstairs and leaves us there.

Keegan is so pale that I'm worried she might pass out. She puts her hand on the rusty doorknob and turns it, struggling for a moment to get it to open.

The room is dark, the light from the hallway illuminating a figure on a bed in the far corner.

"Reece?"

Keegan's voice is barely audible, as if she's hoping this isn't her daughter, that this will turn out not to be true.

"Hmmm?"

The girl raises up, and suddenly we can see her face. I hear Keegan gasp, a hand going to her mouth. "Reece," she says. "Oh, Reece." And she starts to cry.

*

Innocence deserves our protection.
– Author Unknown

Keegan

I DROP TO MY knees beside the dirty bed on which my daughter is curled in a fetal position. I put my hand to her forehead and push the oily hair away from her face.

She tries to force her eyes open, but it is as if they are weighted with lead, and the effort is more than she can manage. "Mom?" she says in a raspy voice.

"Yes," I say. "Reece. What have you taken?"

She shakes her head a little, and it's clear she doesn't want to tell me.

Bowie puts his hand on my shoulder, leans in close to my ear and says, "This looks like a meth house."

I hear the words, and yet it feels impossible that my child could be here in a place like this. Anger shoots up from my mid-section, and I want to snap at Bowie, tell him he's wrong. But I can't because I know in my heart he's right.

"Reece," I say softly. "We're going to take you somewhere to get help. But you said something about a baby. What were you talking about?"

Reece moans as if she's just remembered. Tears leak from her eyes and start down her face. "He took him."

"Him?"

"My baby."

"You had the baby?"

She nods once, and a dam of emotion breaks free in my chest. I start to sob beneath its onslaught and the certainty that my daughter had not gone through with the abortion. "Reece. Why didn't you let me help you?"

"I should have," she says. "I'm so sorry, Mommy."

It's been forever since she's called me this. It seems like several lifetimes ago. I clasp her hand between mine, wanting nothing more than to give her a lifeline, to pull her up from this dark place and the dark thing that has a hold on her.

"Who took him, Reece?"

"Tony. He makes meth here. I owed him money. He said he was going to sell the baby to some attorney, that he would be adopted by a couple who would pay a lot to have him and would give him a good life."

My stomach feels as if it has dropped from a hundred stories. Sickness overwhelms me. "What's the baby's name, Reece?"

"Griffith. I called him Griff."

I feel a desperation I have never before felt in my life. Not even when I had two young children of my own and was so broke that I didn't know how I would feed them their next meal. I am suddenly frantic with the need to find this child before something awful happens to him.

I look up at Bowie, knowing all of this is reflected in my eyes, but unable to filter it. "Can you help us find him? Please, Bowie. Please."

*

What do we live for, if not to make life less difficult for each other?

– George Eliot

Bowie

LOOKING DOWN AT Keegan, seeing the helplessness on her face takes me back to the place I have been in so many times. That place of knowing something horrible had happened to a good person through no fault of their own. And being unable to change the fact that the odds were good there would be no way to right that wrong.

And yet I've never wanted to do so more than I do right now.

I force my mind to the state of calm that allows for figuring out what to do next. It means I have to force the emotion from my decision making, disregard what I feel for Keegan, and the empathy I have for the loss she is facing.

My voice is low and even when I say, "First, we should get your daughter out of this place. We'll find a rehab and take her there. Then I'll start making calls about the baby. Can you get her dressed and downstairs? I'll go out and research local rehabs on my phone."

"Yes," she says. "I can do that."

I turn to leave the room, but she stops me with a hand on my arm. "Thank you, Bowie. Thank you."

IN THE CAR, I get busy searching online for rehabs, quickly checking reviews and comments from various sites in an effort to find the one most able to deal with Reece's meth addiction. It's a devil of an addiction, and, at best, she will have a painful road ahead of her.

Within five minutes, I've found what looks like a good place for her. I call the number and ask for an emergency placement. I tell the soft-spoken representative who addresses my questions that Reece's mother will be bringing her to the facility. She says that will be fine and they will be expecting us.

The door to the broken-down house opens, and Keegan appears with Reece, her arm around her shoulder. She's helping her to walk. Reece's head is drooped forward under the effects of whatever she took last.

I get out of the Rover and run to meet them. "I'll carry her," I say, scooping the girl up in my arms and walking to the vehicle. She must weigh ninety pounds or less. I place her in the back seat, buckling her seatbelt at her waist. Her head drops back against the headrest. She's barely conscious.

Keegan gets in the passenger seat, and I jump in the driver's side, turning the GPS on with the address of the rehab. "I found a place about twenty minutes from here," I say to Keegan. "They said to bring her in."

Keegan looks at me then with such gratitude that I realize again how completely overwhelmed she is with what is happening.

"How will I ever thank you?" she asks.

"You don't need to," I say, forcing myself not to think of all the things that can go wrong from here.

*

Find a place inside where there's joy, and the joy will burn out the pain.

– Joseph Campbell

Keegan

THE REHABILITATION CENTER is a pleasant-looking building, brick and stone with lots of landscaping and bright-colored flowers that label it as a happy place.

But I feel anything other than happy at the prospect of leaving Reece here. At the same time, I know I have no other choice. She is in such bad shape.

Bowie pulls up to the front entrance, looking at me with his serious blue eyes. "I'll help you get her inside," he says. "And then I'll come back out and start making calls about the baby."

I nod and get out, knowing if I try to speak, the words will never make it past the tears threatening to spill out of me.

Bowie comes around and opens the back door, reaching in to lift Reece out. Her head lolls back and she makes a sound of protest.

"Where are you taking me?"

The question is barely audible. I take her hand as we walk through the main doors, telling her, "To get you the help you need, Reece. This is where you need to be right now."

She squeezes my hand hard, murmuring, "Griff. Griff."

ADMITTING REECE TO this place is one of the hardest things I've ever done in my life. Somehow, I manage to get her to agree to the admission. She's able to sign the papers she needs to sign, and I'm grateful for that. She's nineteen, and this has to be voluntary.

Bowie disappeared shortly after the woman at the front desk began helping us. I'm praying he's able to get the police to start looking for the baby.

I'm not sure I've even fully processed this fact yet.

Reece has a baby.

How has she taken care of him? Is he all right? Was she on drugs while she was pregnant?

I steer my thoughts away from the questions because I have no idea what to do with them. I focus instead on answering the questions the admissions attendant is asking me. What kind of substance has Reece been abusing? How long has she been doing so?

I have no real answers for her. Only guesses and possibilities. She is sympathetic, as if I'm not the first parent to sit in this chair in a similar position.

"The detox process for methamphetamine addiction is quite unpleasant," she says, the edges of the words blurred with her soft southern accent.

"What are the symptoms?" I ask, concern for Reece flaring inside me.

"Of course they vary patient to patient and will also depend on the length of use and addiction. Typical symptoms are vomiting, depression, and thoughts of suicide. Extreme irritation and anger are also common."

"That sounds horrible," I say.

"It's not an easy process to get through," the woman says, her expression sympathetic. "The doctors can help manage the symptoms with anti-anxiety medications. They can also offer some really good anti-nausea medicines to help with that. And depending on your daughter's weight and blood work results, they might also give her intravenous vitamins and nutrients as well."

"That sounds good," I say, realizing there is nothing good about any of this.

As if she's read my thoughts, she says, "We really try to do everything that can be done to help get the patient through the most difficult parts of the detox. But in truth, symptoms can go on for months after quitting the drug."

"Such as?"

"In extreme cases, amphetamine psychosis can occur. This is similar to schizophrenia in its effects. The patient can have sensations of bugs crawling under their skin, seeing things that aren't there. But let's hope that's not the case for Reece."

At the sound of her name, Reece jerks her head up. "Where am I, Mom?"

"You're in a hospital, Reece," I say, taking her hand. "Remember? We're here to get you some help."

She nods a little, and her eyes glaze over once more.

"I'll get a nurse to come with a wheelchair, and we'll get

her settled in her room. Be right back," she says, before disappearing down the hall.

I reach across and take my daughter's hand in mine. And I wonder how we could possibly have ended up in this place. Why I didn't see the warning signs far enough in advance to prevent this from happening. I try to hold back the sob swooping up from deep inside me like a tsunami from the ocean floor. But I can't, and I bend forward, crying for my failures as a mother and all the pain ahead for my daughter.

*

Never ignore a person who loves you, cares for you, and misses you. Because one day, you might wake up from your sleep and realize that you lost the moon while counting the stars.

– Author Unknown

Bowie

I CALL MITCH FIRST. Not because he will be able to work on finding Reece's baby, but because I know he will point me to the best agent to contact.

He answers the phone with, "Did you find her?"

"We did," I say. "Thank you so much, Mitch."

"Is she okay?"

"I don't know. She's in rough shape. Looks like meth addiction."

"Man, I'm sorry. That's bad news."

"Yeah, but there's more. She has a baby. And it looks like the dealer she's been buying from abducted him with the intent of selling him to pay off her drug debt."

"Damn."

"I know. It's been a fast reintroduction to the underbelly of the drug life."

"You need a name," Mitch says.

"I do."

He gives me one.

HER NAME IS Bethany Daniels, and she's based in the Knoxville field office.

She answers my call on the first ring. "Hi, Bowie. Mitch texted me to expect your call. I've heard some good things about your time in the bureau, and I also enjoy your books. How can I help you?"

"Thank you," I say. "I have a friend whose daughter has been involved with a meth dealer here in Knoxville. He's apparently taken her six-month-old son and is planning to sell him to get back what she owes him."

"Good heavens," Bethany says. "Do you have a name?"

I give her the name Reece had given us.

"Any known address?"

"No," I say. "Apparently, he moves around."

"Handy if you don't want to be found," she says.

"Yeah. He sounds like really bad news. I'm afraid if the baby isn't found soon—"

"Let's not go there," she says. "I'm on it, okay. Can I reach you at this number?"

"Yes. And thank you. Really."

"Hey, if I had my way, I'd take the sewage truck and suck up every one of these loser dealers off the streets. They're just parasites."

She hangs up before I can agree or disagree. I sit for a

moment wondering if they will be fast enough in finding him. And what the outcome will be if they aren't.

By the time Keegan walks out to the car, her face solemn and tear-stained, I've decided I'm not willing to wait around to find out.

WE START BACK at the house where we found Reece. The same drugged-out girl who had answered the door earlier appears again, this time less coherent and more buzzed.

"I don't know what you're talkin' about," she slurs. "I never heard of anybody by that name."

I stand right in front of the girl, using intimidation as a playing card. Keegan is to my right, slightly behind me. "So if you haven't heard of him, who's supplying your party favors?"

"Ain't no party around here," she says, looking up at me through slitted eyes.

"Look, a baby's life is at stake, so my patience with your denials is going to run out in approximately two seconds. At that point, I'll pull out my phone and call my friends at your local police station and ask them to come take a look at this house for suspected illegal drug activity. And when I add to that the fact that a baby has been kidnapped by the thug supplying the drugs, they'll be here before you can even think about where to hide your stash."

"Aw, man, come on," she says. "I didn't ask to be involved in any of this. Reece is the one who kept overspending. You can't take drugs you can't pay for."

"I'm sure it took a great deal of experience for you to come by that nugget of wisdom, but again, if you don't tell me where I can find the lowlife who took that baby—"

"All right, all right," she says, holding up an unsteady hand. "He moves around, but the last I heard he was staying with an old girlfriend. Over on Cedar Street. It's the house at the end of the cul-de-sac. No grass in the front yard and an old Chevelle on blocks."

"Charming," I say. "If he's not there, I'll be back."

She gives me a look that wouldn't bode well for me if she had a gun in her hand. I step back just as she slams the door.

I take Keegan's hand, and we run back to the car, aware that every minute has become precious.

*

We are made wise not by the recollection of our past, but by the responsibility for our future.

– George Bernard Shaw

Keegan

BOWIE ALL BUT ignores the speed limits as we tear down street after street, following the GPS directions. It's only ten minutes away, but it seems as if it takes forever to get there.

We finally reach Cedar Street, and Bowie swings a hard left into the driveway. I start to open my door, but he puts a hand on my arm to stop me.

"Keegan, stay here. Let me go to the door."

"What if he's dangerous? I can't ask this of you—"

"You're not asking." He reaches under the driver's seat and pulls out a gun.

"You brought that with you?" I ask, shocked.

"Old habits," he says.

"Bowie, wait—"

But he's already out the door, slipping the gun beneath his jacket.

The house looks like something out of the worst neighborhood you can imagine. The roof is missing huge chunks of tile. The chimney is slightly askew, as if someone climbed a ladder and took a sledge hammer to it. The paint—a mock cheerful sky blue—is peeling in wide swatches, revealing a dirty white beneath.

My heart is pounding so hard I can hear its drumbeat in

my ears. My palms instantly begin to sweat. I watch, numb, as Bowie knocks at the rusty metal door.

Upstairs, I glimpse someone pulling back a curtain and peering down at the front stoop. The curtain quickly closes, and I suddenly fear that they might run out the back with the baby.

I jump out of the Rover, calling to Bowie. "Upstairs. Someone's there! Should I go around the house?"

"Keegan, no! I'm going in. Stay where you are!"

But he might as well have ordered me to turn myself to stone, because there is no way I can stay here while he goes in, risking his life.

Playing my hunch, I run as fast as I can around the house, tripping over a tree root and barely catching myself before I hit the ground. I'm up though and charging to the backyard, thankful there's no fence.

I hear a door squeak open, footsteps on concrete, and just as I round the corner of the house, I see a skinny guy with long, greasy hair bolting down the sidewalk, a baby boy under his arm like a football. The baby is crying.

I scream out of pure terror, running after him with every ounce of energy I can push through my body. I grab for his jacket, miss, lunge again and get his hair. I hold on, its oily length the only thing between me and losing this child who belongs to my daughter.

I hear Bowie behind me then. I wonder if he's going to tackle the guy, then realize he can't because of the baby. But Bowie runs out ahead, stopping dead in front of him, the gun pointed squarely at his chest.

"Stop," he says, his expression pure steel.

He does. Like a statue. I've still got his hair, so his head is tipped back slightly, and he's looking up instead of directly at Bowie.

"Give the baby to her," Bowie says.

"Who the hell are you?" he asks, his voice a razor edge of rage above the baby's screams.

"Reece is my daughter," I say. "You've kidnapped my grandson. Give him to me now."

"Your angel daughter," he says, disgust underlining each word, "owes me ten thousand dollars. You think I'm supposed to just write off her debt?"

"I don't give a damn what she owes you," Bowie says. "The FBI is on the way to this address right now. You can give us the baby and get out of here, or we can wait with me pointing this gun at your head until they arrive. I'm fine either way. I'm also happy to pull the trigger."

I hear in Bowie's voice something I haven't seen in him before. I remember what he'd told me about why he'd left the FBI, the point of disgust he'd reached with the type of person he'd so often been charged with finding. People with no regard for life, no respect for others.

I release my hold on the guy's hair enough so that he can look at Bowie. I ache to reach for the baby, grab him from this scum bucket's arm, pull him to me, and assure him that he's safe.

But I'm afraid to do anything for fear that he will drop the baby.

"Which one is it?" Bowie asks.

I sense the guy's tensing, and I dread his answer.

Silence hangs between us, and if it is possible to feel hatred like a wave of heat, I feel his.

"Fuck you!" The words explode into the silence, and all of a sudden, I see the baby flying high into the air.

I scream, lunging forward with my arms outstretched. Oh, dear God, please, dear God, don't let him fall! I'm tripping, stumbling, going down on the sidewalk with my arms still outstretched, reaching for the baby, even as I know I am not able to catch him.

*

Out of this nettle, danger, we pluck this flower, safety.
– William Shakespeare

Keegan

I SLIDE ON the concrete, my chin slamming hard into the uneven surface. I hear the baby's cries, trying to scramble to my feet. And then I see that Bowie has caught him. He has him in his arms, tucked tight against his chest, his gun at his feet.

I start to cry and reach to take him. Bowie hands him to me, grabs his gun and starts running after the dealer.

"Bowie, don't!" I call out after him. "Let him go!"

But I know that he won't. That he can't. I drop to my knees, looking down at the innocent face of this child my daughter has brought into the world. He is looking up at me with wide blue eyes that are wet with tears, but he has stopped crying. He holds his little hand up, and I put my finger against his palm. He squeezes it tightly, and I say, "You're safe, sweet boy. You're safe."

*

When you've got it coming, it'll get there sooner or later.
– Author Unknown

Bowie

MY ONLY HOPE is that his punk-ass, drug-addicted self will give out of gas before I do. But he's holding out better than I would have expected.

At first, he sticks to the sidewalks, running fast and straight, but as I gain on him, he cuts through a yard, jumps a short fence, and hits an alleyway that runs between houses.

I clear the fence and follow him, pushing myself to pick up speed. Our footsteps pounding the asphalt along with our ragged breathing are the only sounds.

I could shoot him. Stop dead, aim, and shoot him. Part of me wants to. Part of me knows I would find satisfaction in making sure he never gets another girl addicted, never terrorizes another child.

But that's the part of me that made me realize I had to get out of law enforcement. My own desire to see justice meted out on thugs like this one began to overrule my patience for trusting the system.

So I run harder, fast enough that my heart is pounding against the wall of my chest. As I hoped, he starts to slow, his drugged-out body beginning to fail him.

Another ninety seconds, and he's going down, rolling hard

into the asphalt. I jump him, and we tumble into the grass at the side of the path.

He grunts, yelling, "Get off me, man!"

I wish I had handcuffs, but since I don't, I decide I'll just sit on him until help arrives. I pull my cell phone from my pocket, dialing 911. As I wait for the answer, I decide it's a good day to be six-three.

In time of test, family is best.
– Burmese Proverb

Evan

WHEN MOM'S NUMBER flashes on my phone screen, I answer fast, my pulse pounding. "I've been worried," I say before she can speak. "You haven't been answering your phone."

"I'm sorry, Ev," she says.

There's something in her voice that makes me instantly scared. "What happened? Did you find her?"

"We did. She's in a rehab center in Knoxville now. She'll need to be there for a while. But I think she's okay with it."

"Did she have a baby?" I ask, almost afraid to hear the answer.

"Yes," Mom says. "A little boy. Evan, he's beautiful."

"Really?" I ask, a sudden knot of emotion in my throat. "Are you bringing him home?"

"We are. Could you make a trip to Target and get some things for him?"

"Sure," I say. "Oh, man, I have a nephew."

"You do." I hear the smile in Mom's voice, and it's only then that I realize I haven't heard her sound this way in a really long time. Like our world has a chance of being right again. That maybe Reece is going to be okay after all.

"Can you text me a list of what you need? And is it all right if Analise goes with me?"

"Sure. And Bowie says you can take his truck."

"Cool."

"Are the dogs okay?"

"They're great," I say. "Living the good life."

"Good," she says. "I can't wait to see them. We'll be there around eight or nine tonight."

"Okay. See you then."

"Bye, Evan."

"Hey, Mom?"

"Yeah?"

"I love you."

"I love you too, Ev."

*

Love is all the motivation we need.
– Author Unknown

Keegan

IT FEELS LIKE a dream.

Griffin asleep in a bassinet next to my bed. I doubt that I will actually sleep tonight because I keep rising up to look at him, make sure he's all right.

I know he is what Reece is fighting for. He is what will get her through the awful moments when she will want to leave that facility and give in to the drug that has taken her brain hostage.

I will protect him with my own life. I look at him and see Reece as she had been at his age. I believe with all my heart that she can beat the addiction. She has the will, and this child is her motivation.

And he will be here for her when she is ready. We will be here for her when she is ready.

*

I'll wait for you.
– Joe Nichols

Bowie

I AM BONE-TIRED, but wide awake.

I feel the way I used to feel following an arrest I had been after for a long time. So fueled with adrenaline that it would take days to come back down enough to fall asleep at night in my regular pattern.

Maybe it's because my brain insists on playing back not only what had happened, but all the scenarios that could have caused a completely different outcome.

I keep thinking about how close I came to not catching Griffin before he hit the ground. How easily that sorry excuse for a human being could have gotten out the back door and escaped. That he very well might have if Keegan hadn't grabbed him.

I think too about the look in her eyes when we had taken the baby to the rehab center so that Reece could see him. So much pain for her daughter mixed with hope that she will find her way out of the grip of addiction.

My phone rings.

I fumble for it on the nightstand, see Keegan's name on the screen. "Hey," I say.

"Hey. Were you sleeping?"

"No. You?"

"No," she says. "Can't seem to turn my brain off."

"Me either," I say.

We're both quiet for a couple of moments, and then she says, "How do I ever thank you?"

"You don't owe me any thanks."

"Bowie. You risked your life for us."

"And didn't you save mine not too long ago?"

"That's different."

"How so?"

"I didn't have to chase down a meth dealer to help you out."

I laugh a little. "I actually think it was kind of good for me."

"Good for you?"

"I got to revisit my past and remember why I was right to leave it."

"Can I just say you were darn impressive?"

"If you insist," I say, teasing.

She laughs. And we're silent again. But it's a good silence, two people comfortable with each other. Aware of the connection between them.

"Can I ask you something?" she finally says.

"Anything."

"Life is going to be a little crazy for a while. But once it settles down a bit, do you think we could see what this thing between us might be?"

"You mean like spend some time together?"

"Some serious time," she says softly.

"Should I pretend like I need to check my calendar?"

"Only if you need to play hard to get."

"I don't think I do."

"Oh, good. So I'll pencil you in sometime in August?"

"Would I sound overeager if I said I'll be waiting by the phone?"

"I like overeager." There's a smile in her voice.

"I can definitely give you eager."

"I can't wait," she says.

"In August then," I say.

"In August."

*

It might take a year, it might take a day, but what's meant to be will always find its way.
– Author Unknown

Keegan

August 8th

IT FEELS AS if I've never been on a date before.

I can't decide what to wear, and my bed may soon buckle beneath the pile of clothes I have tried on and discarded.

A knock sounds at my bedroom door. "Come in," I call out.

"Wow," Reece says, looking at the bed and smiling.

"Crazy, isn't it?"

"No," she says, walking over to sit down on the corner of the mattress. "You want to look great for Bowie. But you know you could wear a brown paper bag, and he wouldn't be able to quit looking at you."

"I may resort to that bag then," I say, looking at my daughter with a smile on my face. "You look so good, Reece."

She shrugs, not exactly disagreeing. "I feel good," she says.

I walk over to the bed and sit down beside her, tightening the belt to my robe. "You have no idea how grateful I am for how hard you've fought."

"I'm not completely there yet," she says, looking down at her hands.

I smooth my palm across her hair. "I know. But I'm proud of you for where you are."

"I really don't deserve that," she says, looking directly at me without bothering to hide the self-loathing she still struggles with on a daily basis.

"Reece. At some point, you need to decide that it's okay to forgive yourself. You took some wrong turns, but you definitely made some right ones. Look what you've given our family in our precious Griffin."

"He's asleep," she says, her face infusing with sudden light at the mention of his name.

"You mean you got Evan out of his room long enough for that to happen?" I ask with a smile.

"Who knew he'd be such a good uncle?"

"I think they're good for each other."

"Me too." She hesitates, and then, "Mom?"

"Yes, sweetie?"

"I'm sorry for how selfish I was, for trying to make you feel guilty for the things you've accomplished. I don't know why I couldn't see how much you'd given up for Evan and me. I guess having Griffin has made me realize how much you must have sacrificed and how hard it must have been without anyone to help you."

I press my hand against hers. "The past doesn't matter, honey. We're here now. That's all that matters."

"I'm just sorry for hurting you the way I did."

"Thank you," I say because I sense that she needs to be forgiven instead of placated.

"Will you promise me something?"

"What?" I ask.

"That you'll give this thing with Bowie a real shot? You deserve a good man in your life, someone who sees you for you. I think it's pretty clear that he does."

I pull my daughter into my arms, saying softly, "That's a

promise I'm happy to make. Because I do want to give it a real shot. And I'm hoping he feels the same way."

We hug for a long moment, and then Reece stands up. "If you don't get dressed, I might have to go on this date with him."

"I'm on it," I say, jumping up and grabbing a dress off the bed. All of a sudden, I don't really care what I'm wearing. I just want to see him. So much that I can't get ready fast enough.

When I'm done, Reece gives me a look of approval. "You look amazing," she says.

I glance in the mirror, pressing my hands down the front of my dress. "Are you sure this color doesn't make me look—"

"It makes you look gorgeous," she says, grabbing my hand. "Okay, I think he's downstairs. You have to go."

"But my lipstick—"

"Looks fabulous! Come on!"

I follow my daughter down the stairs, and I'm so nervous that it feels as if my face is frozen in place.

"Here she is," Reece announces with pride, as she leads me into the living room.

Bowie is standing by the window that looks out at the lake, talking with Evan. The three dogs are lounging on the rug next to them. Bowie turns at the sound of Reece's voice, his eyes widening at the sight of me.

"Wow," he says. "I'd almost forgotten how beautiful you are."

"Points, Bowie," Evan says, reaching down to rub Noah's head.

I find my smile and say, "Thank you. We worked at it. Or I should say Reece worked at it."

We look at each other then like teenagers trying to

navigate the waters of awkwardness and finding the waves a bit choppy.

"Ready?" he asks.

"Yes," I say.

"Don't worry, Mom," Evan says. "We've got the fort."

"I think he means we'll hold it down while you're gone," Reece says, shaking her head.

"Okay, then," I say.

"I'll have her back by midnight," Bowie says, taking my hand and leading me to the door.

It's the first time I've left the two of them alone with Griffin, and I'm suddenly beset with a bout of worry. "The monitor is on, right?" I call back over my shoulder.

"Monitor's on, Mom," Reece says. "Go have fun."

AND WE DO.

We take Bowie's truck to dinner at the Landing Restaurant. We sit at a table by the window overlooking the marina and the cove where boats motor in and out.

The waitress takes our order, and once we no longer have our menus to focus on, Bowie looks at me and says, "Reece is doing well?"

"She is. It's a daily battle, the addiction. She knows it

though and approaches it that way. But I think it's going to take a long time for her to forgive herself."

"She will though because the people who love her have."

The waitress returns with a glass of wine for us both. I take a sip of mine, and then let myself say what I've wanted to say to him for weeks now. "Do you believe people are meant to meet each other, Bowie?"

He holds my gaze for a moment, and then says, "Yeah. I do."

"There hasn't been anyone in my life for a long time. I stopped wanting to date just for the sake of dating. I kind of started to think I would never meet anyone that—"

"—made it worth the effort?"

I shrug a yes.

He studies me for several long seconds, and then, as if he's sure he's going out on a limb, "I'd like to be that someone, Keegan. I'd like to be the man who makes you believe in love like you've never believed in it before. A man who wants to be your partner in life, who shares your joy and holds you up when there's pain. You don't need a caretaker. You're a strong woman who's made a great life for herself. I'd like to love you. Just that. For the rest of my life, Keegan."

I feel the words wrap themselves around my heart, and something inside me clicks into place. I've waited for him. I know this from the bottom of my soul. I reach across the table and slip my hand into his. Tears well in my eyes, and I smile through them. "Is that a proposal?"

He smiles back at me. "Not the most well-crafted one, but yes," he says, and then adds, "Will you have me?"

I entwine my fingers with his, letting him see my desire for him. "Yes. And I hope it's sooner than later."

His blue eyes deepen with longing. "Want to make out at the top of Smith Mountain before I take you home?"

"Think we could come back for dinner another time?"

"We could," he says, grinning. He signals the waitress, tells her we have to go and pays for our wine.

We get up from the table, and he takes my hand, leading me quickly out of the restaurant. We're laughing as we slide into the truck. Bowie starts it and points it down the road facing Smith Mountain, its tree-lined slope blue green in the evening light. I sit in the middle of the bench seat, still holding his hand. The windows are lowered, and the heated air of a summer night caresses my face and arms.

We turn and follow the gravel road that leads to an entrance at the foot of the mountain. Bowie navigates the truck through the open gate and starts up the rutted road.

I loop my arms around his neck and kiss his cheek, his ear. He runs his hand down my leg and I release a sound of longing that makes his whole body go taut. "Keegan—"

I keep kissing him until he stops the truck and sinks his mouth fully onto mine. I feel as if I have been lit from the inside, my skin instantly blazing hot.

"We're not to the top yet," he says, throwing the truck in park.

I slide my arms around his neck and pull him to me, smiling against his beautiful mouth. "The view from here is just fine."

******

Next in the Smith Mountain Lake Series: Fences

Next in the Smith Mountain Lake Series!

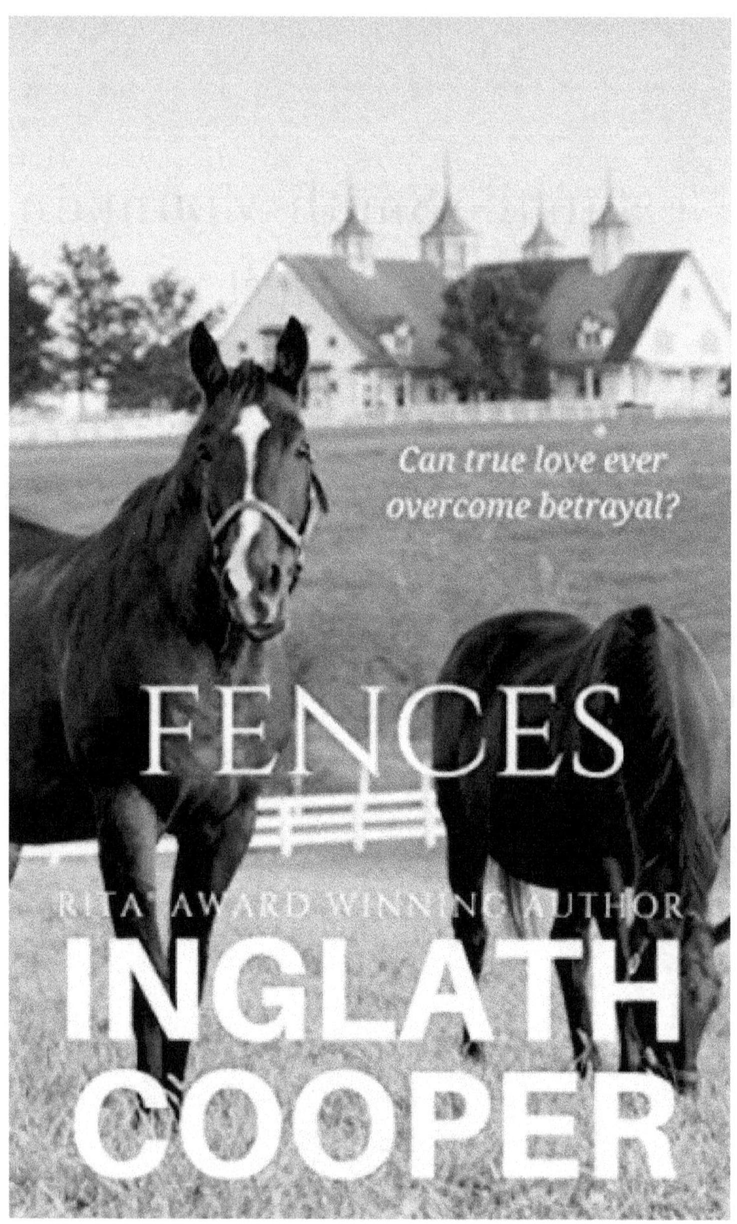

Can true love ever overcome betrayal?

At eighteen, Tate Callahan left Smith Mountain Lake with no intention of ever coming back. The one thing he'd believed in after a lifetime of growing up in foster homes was his love for Jillie Andrews and her love for him. But a single act of jealousy had destroyed all that, and Tate has spent the past eighteen years trying to convince himself what they had was never real. And he's done a pretty good job of it, until the day someone decides the past isn't better left alone. When old accusations are brought to light, Tate believes Jillie is responsible and heads back to Smith Mountain Lake to once and for all prove to himself that she is not the woman of his dreams, but the woman who had destroyed his dreams. What he finds though isn't at all what he'd expected. And the question he will have to answer is whether the protective fences we build around ourselves can ever be taken down, letting us see not only what might have been, but what can still be.

Dear Reader,

I would like to thank you for taking the time to read my story. There are so many wonderful books to choose from these days, and I am hugely appreciative that you chose mine.

Come check out my Facebook page for postings on books, dogs and things that make life good!

Wishing you many, many happy afternoons of reading pleasure.

All best,

Inglath

More Books by Inglath Cooper

Swerve
The Heart That Breaks
My Italian Lover
Fences – Book Three – Smith Mountain Lake Series
Dragonfly Summer – Book Two – Smith Mountain Lake Series
Blue Wide Sky – Book One – Smith Mountain Lake Series
That Month in Tuscany
And Then You Loved Me
Down a Country Road
Good Guys Love Dogs
Truths and Roses
Nashville – Part Ten – Not Without You
Nashville – Book Nine – You, Me and a Palm Tree
Nashville – Book Eight – R U Serious
Nashville – Book Seven – Commit
Nashville – Book Six – Sweet Tea and Me
Nashville – Book Five – Amazed
Nashville – Book Four – Pleasure in the Rain
Nashville – Book Three – What We Feel

Nashville – Book Two – Hammer and a Song
Nashville – Book One – Ready to Reach
On Angel's Wings
A Gift of Grace
RITA® Award Winner John Riley's Girl
A Woman With Secrets
Unfinished Business
A Woman Like Annie
The Lost Daughter of Pigeon Hollow
A Year and a Day

About Inglath Cooper

RITA® Award-winning author Inglath Cooper was born in Virginia. She is a graduate of Virginia Tech with a degree in English. She fell in love with books as soon as she learned how to read. "My mom read to us before bed, and I think that's how I started to love stories. It was like a little mini-vacation we looked forward to every night before going to sleep. I think I eventually read most of the books in my elementary school library."

That love for books translated into a natural love for writing and a desire to create stories that other readers could get lost in, just as she had gotten lost in her favorite books. Her stories focus on the dynamics of relationships, those between a man and a woman, mother and daughter, sisters, friends. They most often take place in small Virginia towns very much like the one where she grew up and are peopled with characters who reflect those values and traditions.

"There's something about small-town life that's just part of who I am. I've had the desire to live in other places, wondered what it would be like to be a true Manhattanite, but the thing I know I would miss is the familiarity of faces everywhere I go. There's a lot to be said for going in the grocery store and seeing ten people you know!"

Inglath Cooper is an avid supporter of companion animal

rescue and is a volunteer and donor for the Franklin County Humane Society. She and her family have fostered many dogs and cats that have gone on to be adopted by other families. "The rewards are endless. It's an eye-opening moment to realize that what one person throws away can fill another person's life with love and joy."

Follow Inglath on Facebook

at www.facebook.com/inglathcooperbooks

Join her mailing list for news of new releases and giveaways at www.inglathcooper.com

Get in Touch with Inglath Cooper

Follow Inglath Cooper Books on Instagram.

Email: inglathcooper@gmail.com
Facebook – Inglath Cooper Books
Instagram – inglath.cooper.books
Pinterest – Inglath Cooper Books
Twitter – InglathCooper

CPSIA information can be obtained
at www.ICGtesting.com
Printed in the USA
LVHW021156090720
660101LV00001B/11

9 780997 341515